Heaven help her!

It was futile to indulge in spinsterish fantasies about a man who might well be a murderer and thief. Delia had come to the bedchamber for only one purpose: to bring the man his clothes and valise. Before she knew what she was about, however, he had caught her around the waist, holding her captive. Then he had kissed her.

When his lips touched her, all her thoughts ceased, leaving only her senses to do battle. Not that they fought very hard. Not when the warmth of his body against hers sent tingling sensations skittering down her spine, while the masculine, sleepy smell of him filled her in a dizzying way no champagne could match. Then there was the taste of him. . . .

Beware, her saner self cautioned, *for before you lies certain danger. . . .*

An
Inconvenient Heir

Martha Kirkland

A SIGNET BOOK

SIGNET
Published by New American Library, a division of
Penguin Putnam Inc., 375 Hudson Street,
New York, New York 10014, U.S.A.
Penguin Books Ltd, 80 Strand,
London WC2R 0RL, England
Penguin Books Australia Ltd, 250 Camberwell Road
Camberwell, Victoria 3124, Australia
Penguin Books Canada Ltd, 10 Alcorn Avenue,
Toronto, Ontario, Canada M4V 3B2
Penguin Books (N.Z.) Ltd, 182–190 Wairau Road,
Auckland 10, New Zealand

Penguin Books Ltd, Registered Offices:
Harmondsworth, Middlesex, England

First published by Signet, an imprint of New American Library,
a division of Penguin Putnam Inc.

First Printing, January 2003
10 9 8 7 6 5 4 3 2 1

 REGISTERED TRADEMARK—MARCA REGISTRADA

Printed in the United States of America

PUBLISHER'S NOTE
This is a work of fiction. Names, characters, places, and incidents either are
the product of the author's imagination or are used fictitiously, and any resem-
blance to actual persons, living or dead, business establishments, events, or
locales is entirely coincidental.

BOOKS ARE AVAILABLE AT QUANTITY DISCOUNTS WHEN USED TO PROMOTE
PRODUCTS OR SERVICES. FOR INFORMATION PLEASE WRITE TO PREMIUM MAR-
KETING DIVISION, PENGUIN PUTNAM INC., 375 HUDSON STREET, NEW YORK, NEW
YORK 10014.

For William Bryan Knotts, a lover of the outdoors, a woodworker, and a maker of clay and model figures. And to the ladies who loved him: Amber, Shanna, and Annette.

Chapter One

Ems Regis, West Sussex,
May, 1811 . . .

After taking a fortifying breath, Delia Barrington dipped the freshly sharpened quill into the small tin of ink, then carefully tapped the nib against the neck of the tin to remove any excess liquid. During the past two months, she had written this letter at least a thousand times in her mind, but this was her first attempt at actually putting the words on paper. As she prepared to write, her hand shook.

She was afraid. Truly afraid, and she needed help. She had taken care of others for so long, she had almost forgotten how to take care of herself. Of course, there was still Robbie. The baby needed her for just a little while longer, just until she could deliver him to his grandfather.

Heaven help her after that! And heaven help the little boy once he got to his grandfather's; especially if the rumors were true.

Before she fled London, Delia had heard that Major Mitchell Holcomb was not a man to be crossed. And now, as a result of the cold-blooded murder of his cousin William, the major was the heir presumptive to Sir Allistair Holcomb's title and fortune. Had the major been a party to his cousin's murder? If so, what

if he should intercept this letter informing the baronet
of William's baby?

Sir Allistair's only son was dead. Hopefully, the
baronet would be elated to discover he had a grandson. But what of the major? He had been in the
army since he left university, and now he was thirty
or thirty-one-years old. It would be understandable
if he had grown weary of living on an officer's pay.
Who could say how desperate he might be to step
into his uncle's shoes?

Sir Allistair Holcomb was an elderly man possessing
great wealth and a lovely estate in East Sussex. It was
altogether possible that his nephew would be less than
pleased to discover that there was someone whose
claim was more direct than his own to that wealth and
property. How *inconvenient* would Major Holcomb
find the new heir?

There had already been one murder, and Delia did
not want to be responsible for a second. Not hers. Not
Robbie's. Knowing she would lose her nerve if she
hesitated for another moment, she set quill to paper.

Dear Sir Allistair,
  I pray this letter will reach you and not fall into
the hands of your nephew. I was a friend of
your son's, and a particular friend of Maria
Eskew Holcomb, your son's wife. Yes, his
wife!
  You will be surprised to discover that William
was married. His reasons for keeping the mar-
riage a secret are his own, and I do not judge
him. I merely state the facts. I hope you will
be pleased to know that he and Maria were
happy, and that their union resulted in the birth
of a child, a boy who will soon be eight months
old.
  Sadly, Maria died shortly after giving birth.
Upon the death of his dear wife, William gave

*the newborn into my care, with instructions that
I was to write you should anything happen to
him. As well, he entrusted me with his marriage
lines and certain other papers that are for your
eyes only.*

*For reasons I cannot divulge at this time, I have
been unable to write until now.*

*As you will see from the direction of this letter,
I am presently residing in West Sussex, at Sky
Cottage, a small travelers' rest that is also the
home of Maria's grandmother. Unless I hear
from you otherwise, I plan to travel to Holcomb
Park in a fortnight's time to bring you your
grandson.*

*I beg of you, do not tell anyone about this let-
ter, or that I am coming to you. It is a matter
of the deepest urgency.*

Yrs. most respectfully,
Miss Cordelia Barrington

* * *

"It is a damned humbug!" Major Mitchell Holcomb
said. After giving the letter one last look, he tossed it
onto the ink-stained desk of the aging attorney who
was his uncle's man of affairs.

"I thought so as well," Lester Venton said, "at first.
I told myself that the story was the work of a charlatan, some despicable female who believes she can sep-
arate a bereaved old man from a great deal of his
money."

Mitchell had not missed the "however" that remained unspoken. "And now?"

The lawyer hesitated. "And now I do not know.
After careful consideration, I have concluded only one
thing, that the letter writer is genuinely frightened."

"If she is frightened, I daresay it is of my putting
an end to her little scheme. Otherwise, why was she

so particular in her wish that the letter not fall into my hands?"

The lawyer shook his head. "That I cannot say. But what if she is telling the truth? What if your cousin did, indeed, have a wife and a child?"

The major's thick black eyebrows came together in a scowl. "I promise you, sir, he did not. When I saw William not two weeks before his death, he said nothing to me of any such connections. Granted, he was agitated about something, and kept looking over his shoulder, but would a man have reacted thus about a wife and child?"

"Being a bachelor myself, Major, I cannot say."

"Nor can I. However, William and I were more than cousins. Though six years divided us in age, we were friends, and he would not have kept such news a secret."

Lester Venton removed a linen handkerchief from inside his dull green coat and busied himself polishing his wire-rimmed spectacles. "It has been my experience," he said, "that people keep secrets for any number of reasons."

At the younger man's *humph*, the lawyer attacked the spectacles once again, embarrassed at having to state the obvious. "You have been in the military for some years, I believe."

"Nine years, sir. What has that to say to the matter?"

Venton cleared his throat. "Only this, Major. Though I understand that when you two were lads, Mr. William Holcomb looked up to you as his hero, he has had nine years in which to grow and mature, nine years in which to form interests and loyalties of which you may be totally unaware. Surely I need not tell you that time and separation take their toll upon even the closest of relationships."

"Some relationships, Venton. Not ours."

The attorney watched the tall, broad-shouldered

gentleman stand and begin to pace the small office, adding measurably to the wear of the aging Axminster carpet. A man of action, the visitor obviously found the office confining.

"Did my uncle see this letter?"

"Thankfully, he did not. I had taken the precaution of instructing Sir Allistair's butler to forward all correspondence to this office for handling."

"I am relieved to hear it. Who can say what effect such information would have on a seventy-two-year-old man? Especially one who is so grief stricken he cannot leave his bed."

Without warning, the major stopped his pacing and placed both rather large hands on the surface of the desk, then leaned toward Venton, his face so close the attorney detected a hint of a cleft in the square, uncompromising chin. "I presume you asked me here for a reason, sir. What is it you would have me do? Shall I find this Barrington woman and wring the truth from her scrawny neck?"

Venton swallowed. "Not *wring* it from her, of course. But perhaps . . ."

He let his words trail off, wishing the major would resume his pacing and cease looming over him like a wolf preparing to spring at a hapless sheep. Sir Allistair's nephew was a most intimidating presence, and Venton did not doubt for a moment that the military gentleman had learned early in his career how to use his height and his somewhat imposing figure to good advantage.

A peaceable man, Venton could almost feel sorry for the letter writer, should Major Holcomb choose to extract the truth from her by sheer force of will. And who would know better how to use such force effectively than one who had served with honor in the Peninsula under Sir John Moore, then later under Arthur Wellesley?

True, the major had been wounded eleven months

ago in the battle of Talavera, the wound serious enough to end his military career, but it was obvious that he was still a warrior at heart. For that reason alone, if Miss Cordelia Barrington was the charlatan Major Holcomb believed her to be, she might well rue the day she ever devised this particular scheme.

To the attorney's relief, the military gentleman straightened and began to pace once again.

"This is not even a very original ruse," the major said, "nor is Cordelia Barrington the first female to try her luck with a trumped-up story of a previously unknown heir. Such claims are commonly employed by a certain sort of woman—camp followers and the like—once they discover a soldier has been killed. But ruse it is, and I am just the man to prove it."

Venton studied the gentleman's surprisingly gray eyes; they were filled with determination, and at that moment the lawyer was glad he was not in the unsuspecting Miss Barrington's shoes. Wishful of interjecting a bit of cool logic, he said, "I will admit that using an innocent child for the purpose of extortion is the outside of enough. However, I do advise caution, Major. What if everything the woman says in her letter is true? What if the child is, in fact, Sir Allistair's legitimate grandson?"

"Rest assured, he is not. And I mean to prove it. By the week's end, I will return to this office with the woman's retracted statement in writing."

"Bold words, my friend. I have practiced law for forty years, and in my experience, getting someone to recant is not always easy."

The major's left eyebrow lifted ever so slightly, the simple gesture stating plainly that he was not accustomed to having his word questioned. "After nine years in the army, sir, I have learned how to deal with threats and attempted intimidation, most of it from hardened soldiers who are little better than criminals.

Believe me, bringing a cheeky female to heel should prove to be a simple matter."

The subject apparently exhausted, the lawyer asked Mitchell if he had been to Grosvenor Square, to the town house where his cousin was murdered. "I understood that you meant to go there."

"You understood correctly, sir. I was there earlier today."

Venton hesitated as if reluctant to ask his next question. "Did you discover anything there that might aid in the apprehension of your cousin's murderer?"

"I wish I could answer in the affirmative, sir, but the sad truth is that I discovered nothing more than the authorities have already told us. The house, which once belonged to a Lord Sheffield, was empty. Not even a servant on the premises, though the kitchen, where it is said the murder took place, had been scrubbed clean. Except for the fact that the property now belongs to Lord Sheffield's daughter, who was also absent, I learned nothing."

The lawyer steepled his fingers, then tapped them against his chin, the rhythm obviously helping him think. After several moments of this, however, Mitchell had come to the end of his patience. "What are you thinking, sir?"

"I was wondering, Major, since this Barrington woman says she knew William and has his child in her keeping, if she was in the house at the time of your cousin's murder? If so, she might possess some knowledge of the killer. At the very least, she may know the whereabouts of Lord Sheffield's daughter. In any event, she should be questioned."

Mitchell doubted the would-be extortionist had ever set foot inside the Sheffield town house. Still, if there was the least possibility she might know something that would help bring William's killer to justice, Mitchell had to pursue the matter.

More determined than ever to go to Ems Regis and have a few words with the letter writer, he took his leave of the lawyer. "You may trust the matter to me," he said, retrieving his hat and driving gloves from atop a battered oak file cabinet. "I will deal with Miss Cordelia Barrington."

Chapter Two

*M*itchell halted the spirited bays and climbed down from the curricle. He had always loved this particular section of the West Sussex coast. When his father used to bring him here as a lad, the chalk cliffs had appealed to the adventurous aspect of his nature, for without a word of warning—no fence, no signs—the earth simply dropped away, as if sliced clean by some sword-wielding giant. Each time the young Mitchell had approached the precipice, he had thrilled at the thought that one false step would send him plummeting down the blindingly white cliff, into the blue waters below.

Not that the waters were blue today. The sky was a murky gray, threatening rain, and the Channel reflected the sky. The wind had risen as well, and the brisk sea breeze whipped around Mitchell's face, forcing him to remove his hat or risk having the curly brimmed beaver wrenched from his head and tossed onto the narrow stretch of pebble beach some forty feet below.

At the moment, there was nothing on the beach save a lone stormy petrel that waddled back and forth, playing tag with the incoming tide, and Mitchell had his doubts that the little ebony bird would cease his search for food in order to fetch a stray hat and carry it up the chalky cliff side to its owner. As if to prove

the point, the little petrel took flight, climbing ever
upward until he hitched a ride on an obliging wind
current.

Mitchell found the cool air invigorating, especially
so since he had slept little the past two nights. Since
his departure from London, the saber wound in his
side had been giving him fits, and when that happened,
sleep was as elusive as a rainbow.

He had come to the small fishing village of Ems
Regis to take care of unpleasant business; even so, he
did not regret the trip. To one who loved the sea, it
was reward enough to breathe deeply of the briny
air. Even though Ems Regis was but ten miles from
Chichester, and Chichester was but a short distance
from Fernbourne House, his home, he had not been
here since his return from the Peninsula.

While he stared at the distant whitecaps, a flock of
blue-winged fulmars appeared overhead. The seabirds
flew so close to him their webbed feet were discern-
ible, and though Mitchell enjoyed the magical sight,
the handsome bays—a recent purchase at one of Tat-
tersall's twice-weekly auctions—did not appreciate the
close encounter with their winged brethren. In fact,
those prime bits of blood took exception to the flock's
deafening noise—something between the cackling of
a hen and the quack of a duck—and Mitchell was
obliged to catch hold of the leader's bridle and expend
some real energy to keep the pair under control.

Fortunately, within minutes the fulmars had turned
once again toward the sea.

Though the wind had picked up even more, the
birds were strong and graceful on the wing, and without any seeming movement of their beautifully
rounded pinions, the flock swooped along the Channel
troughs, skimming over the serrated crests and easily
lifting fish right out of the choppy water.

He envied the birds their freedom of movement,
their unfettered lifestyle. They were answerable to no

one, responsible for no one. After nine years of fighting, of taking upon his shoulders decisions that affected other men's lives, Mitchell was exhausted. He craved peace. Quiet. With no personal involvements of any kind. No attachments. No one needing him.

He could think of no better life than to emulate the seabirds. But not today. Today he had business at Sky Cottage. After taking one last look at the waters of the Channel, Mitchell climbed back aboard the curricle and gave the bays the office to be on their way.

From a distance, the village of Ems Regis looked much as Mitchell remembered it, with a single high street flanked by about a dozen one- and two-story shops and lodgings. He also remembered the bridge. Before a person reached the village proper, there was a narrow wooden bridge to be crossed.

Twice a day, at the high tides, the waters of the Channel flooded the area surrounding the village. The rising waters were an ever-present threat to strangers to the district, and during high tide, the bridge—which had been thrown up as a temporary measure across a ravine, then forgotten for at least half a century—was the only route into Ems Regis.

Not wanting to upset the horses even more by forcing them across the rickety bridge, Mitchell shouted to a youth of about twelve who appeared to be headed to the village. "You there," he yelled. "A moment please."

The lad wore a wooden yoke across his shoulders, from which were suspended two buckets filled to the brim with freshly caught fish. The load appeared heavy, and raindrops had begun to fall on the boy's bare head, but curiosity bade him hurry toward the curricle. "Aye, sir," he said. "Be ye lost?"

Mitchell shook his head. "Not yet. I wish to stop at a place called Sky Cottage. It is a travelers' rest of some sort. Do you know it?"

The boy eyed him suspiciously. "I know it, think

on. But I bain't fool enough to stop there. It be where the Pikey lives."

"The Pikey?"

" 'Er as sells the potions and reads the palms of them as 'as the price."

Mitchell had grown up in Sussex and was familiar with the local term for a Gypsy, he was just surprised to hear the word now. Surely this Barrington creature was not some old Gypsy hag. "A shilling," he said, removing the coin from inside his waistcoat, "for directions."

The sight of the silver coin had the desired effect, for suddenly the boy was all politeness. "Ye don't want to go through the village, guv'nor. Just follow yonder sandy lane 'til there be a break in the furze. Ye'll see a sign to the left. Sky Cottage be just beyond."

After tossing the coin, which his informant caught in midair, Mitchell thanked the lad, then turned the bays toward the narrow, sandy lane.

" 'Ave a care," the boy yelled after him. "The Pikey reads minds as well as palms. And if 'er don't like what 'er reads, 'er'll cast a spell on ye. Likely turn ye into a toad, 'er will."

Since that last warning ended with a smothered laugh, Mitchell did not take it seriously. Eager to be on his way, he merely waved his hand to the boy, not bothering to look back.

After cracking his whip in the air above the reluctant horses' heads, he maneuvered the curricle down the narrow lane, which was bordered on both sides by yellow gorse, or furze, and tall, spindly sea grasses. Thankfully, within a matter of minutes he spied the break in the furze. As promised, to the left was a post bearing a small wooden sign that read SKY COTTAGE, and beyond that, all but hidden behind a ten-foot hedge that was an impossible tangle of hawthorn, brambles, and gorse stood a two-story cottage.

Built at least two centuries earlier, the flint and mortar cottage was typical of Sussex, possessing a Horsham stone slate roof whose sides reached all the way to the ground. Though not large, the cottage appeared well cared for, with two dormer windows abovestairs and two casements below, situated on either side of the entrance door. All four windows were glazed, and each was hung with thick wooden shutters to guard against the harsh winds that sometime blew in from the Channel.

For an instant, Mitchell thought he spied a face in one of the dormers, as if someone was watching him, but a sudden flash of lightning, followed by a distant clap of thunder, put all from his mind save finding a protected place to tie the horses.

"Around here," yelled an old woman who seemed to have appeared from nowhere.

All but obscured by a thick woven shawl she'd thrown over her head to protect her from the weather, she waved Mitchell toward the back of the cottage. He was quick to obey her signal, for the rain was now coming down with a vengeance, dumping an ocean of water on him. Thankfully, when he reached the area behind the cottage he was rewarded with the sight of a stable, small but sufficient to shelter two horses.

He unfastened the bays, working with all due speed, then led them inside, settling them in the two clean stalls where fresh water and hay had been provided, almost as if someone had been expecting them. Some minutes later, when he came back outside and secured the stable door, the storm had grown worse, with the wind making it appear as if the rain was falling sideways.

Mitchell's coat and breeches were already soaked through, but now what felt like buckets of water ran directly into his top boots. Wet from head to toe and ever mindful of the ache in his side, he hurried back around to the front of the cottage, happy to find the door standing open. Without hesitating, he stepped inside, out of the rain.

The interior of the cottage was warm and inviting and smelled pleasantly of herbs and spices, which came as no surprise, for myriad bundles of drying greenery hung from the thick, age-darkened beams of the low ceiling. The instant Mitchell entered the rectangular room that formed the entire lower floor, a frail voice bid him welcome to Sky Cottage.

The speech was heavily accented, as though English was not the speaker's native tongue. "You must be freezing, sir. Pray, go to the fire and warm yourself, while I prepare you a cup of tea."

"Thank you, ma'am, but I—" The words caught in Mitchell's throat, for now that he saw the woman up close, he was reminded of the village boy's warning about being turned into a toad.

She was incredibly old and quite small—possibly no more than four and a half feet tall—and her hair was twisted into a careless bun from which several silvery white strands stood out like sticks protruding from a haystack. Her wrinkled skin was the texture of parchment and the color of weak tea, and she resembled nothing so much as one of those ancient witches of lore—the type of child-stealing crone nursery maids invoked to frighten recalcitrant children into obedience.

The Pikey, Mitchell thought.

Small, bare feet showed beneath a faded, ankle-length green skirt, and to further underscore the image of a Gypsy, the old woman wore the traditional kerchief around her neck. Several noisy bracelets clinked against one another at her wrists, while loops containing gold coins hung from her rather pendulous earlobes. As well, every finger on her thin, age-spotted hands bore a ring.

"Go to the fire," she said again, her smile revealing a missing front tooth. "You can stare at me as well from there."

Mitchell chuckled. "Your pardon, ma'am. I seem to have forgotten my manners."

Ignoring his apology, she said, "Two shillings for the night, plus a light supper. An additional sixpence if you want the horses fed and watered as well. Tuppence if you do the job yourself."

For the moment, Mitchell had forgotten that the cottage was also a travelers' rest. "I have not come to stay. I wish to speak to a Miss Cordelia Barrington. Is that you?"

The old woman's smile vanished instantly. "Nay. Nadja Eskew is my name."

Eskew? According to the letter, that was also the name of William's supposed wife. Was this Maria's grandmother? If so, it should prove conclusively that the entire marriage story was a fraud, for William would never have aligned himself with the family of this Gypsy innkeeper. William knew how ardently Sir Allistair wished him to make a brilliant match, and as a dutiful son, he would never have disappointed his father by entering into a *mesalliance.*

"What business have you with Miss Barrington?" the old woman asked.

"She sent a letter to Holcomb Park, and—"

"But not to you, I think."

Mystified by her sharp retort, Mitchell was slow to reply. "No, not to me. The letter was meant for my uncle."

"Then, perhaps it is your uncle who should have come."

Before he could explain that his uncle was unwell, the old crone motioned toward the narrow wooden stairs that gave access to the upper floor. "Above stairs," she said. "The chamber to the right, at the rear. Go there, and I will bring your tea."

Mitchell hesitated for a moment, pondering the wisdom of going abovestairs, away from the easy access of the entrance door. What if the old woman was deranged? "I told you," he said, "that I do not mean to stay."

As if she had not heard him, she turned to an ancient oak dresser from which she removed a small crockery jar and a cup and saucer. After placing the cup and saucer on a well-scrubbed deal table that obviously served as both work surface and dining area, she measured out a spoonful of dark powder from the jar, dumped the powder into the cup, then hurried over to the cavernous fireplace, where a kettle sat on the hob just off the flames. Using care, she poured steaming water into the cup, then stirred the contents slowly.

"Abovestairs," she said again. "I will bring the tea."

Though he hesitated a second time, Mitchell felt just a bit foolish for doing so. After all, what possible harm could this little dab of a woman do to a man his size? Furthermore, this was a travelers' rest, and he was a traveler, cold and tired and in need of a short respite. If the truth be known, he had been wondering this half hour and more how much longer he could remain on his feet. A bit of privacy would be welcome, and unless he missed his guess, the rain had set in for the afternoon and the roads would soon be muddy quagmires.

Since the woman he came to see was nowhere in sight, he might as well make himself as comfortable as possible while he waited for Nadja Eskew to fetch her. The decision made, he climbed the narrow stairs to the upper floor.

As he had expected, two bedchambers faced to the front and two to the rear. "To the right," the old woman said.

Mitchell started, for he had not expected her to follow so close behind him. For such an elderly person, she was surprisingly spry. "Go on in," she said. "But mind your head."

After thanking her for saving him from a painful

encounter with the low lintel above the doorway, Mitchell lifted the latch, ducked, then stepped just inside the room. It was a small chamber, with a narrow wood-frame bed tucked beneath the low-pitched, sloping slate roof, and the only other furniture a ladder-back chair with a cane seat and an oak chest of drawers that held a tin washbasin and a pewter candlestick.

The old Gypsy laid her hand on Mitchell's forearm, as if to urge him farther into the room. The instant her be-ringed fingers touched his wet sleeve, however, she drew back her hand, as though she had touched something repellent. Her eyes, already as black as two lumps of coal, seemed to grow even blacker, and for a moment Mitchell thought he saw anger in their depths. Though what she had to be angry about, he could not even guess.

"Drink this," she said quietly, passing him the cup and saucer. "It will warm you."

The steam that rose from the mahogany-colored liquid was tangy and inviting, the aroma tempting, and not wanting to insult the woman by refusing her hospitality, Mitchell lifted the cup to his lips and sipped. "Umm," he murmured. "Delicious."

Without further prompting, he drank every last drop, and immediately began to feel the warming effects of the tasty brew.

"You would be wise," Nadja Eskew said, "to remove your wet things. All of them, mind you, then wrap yourself in the coverlet from the bed. I will return directly to take the clothes down to the fire to dry." After a moment's hesitation, she added, "Stretch out on the bed, for then your wound will be less painful."

His wound? Mitchell stared at her. Could the old Gypsy really read minds? If not, then how the deuce did she know he had been wounded? Or that his left side hurt like hell?

Even after eleven months, the long, jagged scar was

still tender where the Frenchman's sword had plunged through the skin, the angry thrust breaking two of Mitchell's ribs and narrowly missing his lungs. For the past half hour, the icy state of his clothing had dulled the pain, but now, with the warmth inside the cottage, the wound had begun to throb like the drums of Hades.

Though curious as to how the old crone knew so much about him, he did not give voice to his question. Instead, once she left the room, he did the logical thing and began to remove his wet clothes, starting with his boots. No point in contracting an inflammation of the lungs just to prove how resilient he was. He had learned in the army that stubbornness in such matters could be fatal.

Oddly, his movements felt unusually slow, as if his energy was evaporating bit by bit, until even the simplest motion required great effort on his part. Only through concentration did he manage to unbutton his sodden coat, remove it and the waistcoat, tug his linen shirt over his head, and peel the snug tan breeches down his legs.

After tossing each of the wet items across the straight-backed chair, he reached for the many-colored, quilted coverlet and wrapped it around his naked body like a Greek toga. That simple task left him feeling weaker than he wanted to admit, and to keep from falling, he sat on the edge of the narrow bed. The old woman had suggested that he make use of the bed, and though the feather-filled mattress was too short for a man of his height, he succumbed to temptation and stretched out, barely even noticing when the wood frame groaned with his weight.

The instant his head touched the down-filled pillow, he forgot everything save the heaviness of his eyelids. Once, thinking that he should make the effort, he tried to raise his feet, where they hung off the end of the bed. To his dismay, not even his bare toes would obey his command to wiggle. Nor, for that matter, could he lift his arms, and had he not felt it to be an idiotic notion, he might have suspected that he had been drugged. Pure foolishness, of course, for why would anyone wish to render him unconscious?

As if from a great distance, Mitchell heard whispered voices, muffled by the wall that divided the two back bedchambers. "He is not the one you fear," the old woman said. "But have a care, *Pisliskurja Sedra*, for there is much anger in him."

"I will be on my guard." The second voice was younger, the speech refined. "Thank you, *Phuri daj.*"

Though they addressed one another by Romany names, the second voice was unaccented. The younger woman said something else, but Mitchell was unable to hear it clearly.

From somewhere, he thought he heard a baby cry, but he could not be certain of anything, for the sounds had become distorted, as though he had packed cotton wool in his ears.

Soon his eyelids grew so heavy he could no longer force them open. He was drifting to sleep. Drifting. Drifting. His body felt so light it seemed to float on air; effortlessly, like the seabirds floating over the Channel. Within the space of a sigh, he knew nothing more.

Delia stood quietly, watching the sleeping child whose tiny, rosebud lips moved slightly, as if he still suckled. He had been fretful all morning from the distress of teething, and it had taken her longer than usual to get him settled in his cot for his afternoon nap. Once he was asleep, however, that miracle happened and he was again her precious angel. At the mere sight of him, with the soft blond curls that begged to be touched and the skin of his cheeks so unbelievably smooth they defied description, something stirred deep inside Delia.

Unable to stop herself, she bent and kissed his fore-head, letting his precious baby fragrance fill her nos-trils. "Sleep well, little one," she whispered. "I promised to keep you safe, and I shall never fail you. No matter what it takes."

After closing the bedchamber door, she descended the narrow stairs slowly. She looked all around the large room, expecting to see the man Nadja Eskew had warned her about, but to her surprise, she saw no one save the old woman, who was busy chopping on-ions for the evening stew. "Nadja?"

Anticipating the question, Nadja said, "The man is asleep."

"Asleep? But—"

"I made him some of my special tea."

"What!"

Delia stared at the baby's great-grandmother. "You drugged the man? But why, *Phuri daj*? If he has come in answer to my letter, surely Sir Allistair sent him to escort us to Holcomb Park."

The old woman shook her head. "This one does the bidding of no man. He is a leader, not a follower. A soldier. And he means you no good."

A soldier! Like an animal caught in a trap, Delia's heart tried to escape her chest. *Major Holcomb.* She drew a ragged breath. *It could be none other.* "Are you quite certain?"

Nadja's black eyes lifted from her task, the onions forgotten. "You doubt me?"

"No, no. I trust your powers, *Phuri daj*."

Delia should not have questioned Nadja's pro-nouncement, for the woman was a *taibhsear*—a seer of visions. If Nadja Eskew said the man meant her no good, it was true. "Earlier you said he had much anger in him. If that is true, then it can mean only one thing—that Major Holcomb does not wish Robbie taken to his grandfather."

"He does not wish it," Nadja said. "That I know to be true."

The pronouncement, coming from a woman with Nadja's insight, sounded ominous, causing Delia's knees to shake so badly she was obliged to seek the wooden settle beside the fireplace. "If he has not come to be of assistance, can it be that he . . . do you suspect the major of wanting to—"

"When it comes to my great-grandson," she said, not needing to hear the rest of Delia's question, "I trust no one. Robbie stands between Major Holcomb and a sizeable inheritance. I do not need to tell you there are men who would commit murder for less."

No. She did not need to be told about murderers. Furthermore, to deny the truth of Nadja's statement would be to put Maria's baby in serious danger. Delia disliked thinking a grown man would threaten an infant's safety, but since witnessing the brutal and unprovoked murder of William Holcomb—in her own kitchen!—she had lost all faith in humankind.

She had fled London to protect herself from the cold-eyed little man in black—the unknown villain who had shot William—and for the past two months she had remained hidden, fearful for her own life. Now it would appear that hers might not be the only life in danger.

After licking suddenly dry lips, Delia turned to the baby's great-grandmother. "What am I to do, Nadja? We cannot let anything happen to Robbie."

"We will not do so. My people are camped only a few miles from here. For days I have been thinking it is time I visited them, to show them my great-grandson."

"Will the Roms accept him?"

Nadja smiled. "They will call him a little *raklo*, but they will accept him because he is flesh of my flesh. And," she added, "for that same reason they will protect us with their lives."

For just a moment, Delia wished she could go with Nadja and the baby. She had not felt safe in such a long time, and after jumping at shadows for the past two months, it would be wonderful to know that a band of men would protect her with their lives. Not that she could ask that of anyone.

As if reading her thoughts, Nadja said, "Come with us, *Pisliskurja Sedra*."

"I cannot, *Phuri daj*. I am being pursued. I feel it." She smiled then. "I may not be a *taibhsear*, but I know the murderer has not given up looking for me. I saw what he did and I saw his face. And had my house-keeper and her formidable-looking suitor not chosen that moment to enter the town house, the murderer would have killed me as well and left my body be-side William's."

The old woman crossed the room, stopping beside the settle. With Delia seated, they looked directly into one another's eyes. "I will gather my things," Nadja said, "then once the moon rises, the little one and I will leave."

When she reached across and kissed Delia's cheek, the younger woman slipped her arms around the old Gypsy's waist, holding her tightly for several moments. "I will miss you."

"*Dili!*" Nadja said, pushing away as if embarrassed by the attachment that had grown between them.

Delia smiled, for though the old woman had called her an idiot, she knew it was meant as an endearment.

Bracelets clanked against one another as Nadja used the backs of her hands to brush away the moisture that spilled from her eyes. "Here," she said, removing the kerchief from around her neck. "When the soldier is gone, hang this *diklo* in the window. Someone will be watching, and when they see the sign, they will know it is safe for me and the little one to return to the cottage."

Not wanting to think about being parted from the

baby she had grown to love, or of being alone once again, Delia concentrated on practicalities. "What of the major's horses?"

"I will see to the team before I leave."

"And the major? What shall I do about him?"

"For now, let him sleep. The potion will last from sun to sun. Longer if the person is sick or tired, and I believe the major is both."

"And tomorrow?"

"Tomorrow, do not forget to collect two shillings from him for the night's lodging. And," Nadja continued, her broad smile adding dozens of creases to her tea-hued face, "an extra sixpence for the special tea."

Chapter Three

*M*itchell was dreaming. He must be.

In years past, he had possessed the happy knack of sleeping in the most unlikely places—a valuable talent for a soldier—but since his injury, peaceful repose had been denied him. Even when he managed to fall asleep, the resulting experience was generally fitful and lasted for no longer than an hour or two at a time. Now he felt unbelievably refreshed, as though he had slept for a fortnight.

Suspecting he might still be asleep, and not wanting to risk breaking the lovely spell that cocooned him in its tranquillity, he opened his eyes the least little bit, just enough to spy the moonlight that cast a pool of silvery brightness on the bare wooden floor to the left of the narrow bed. Just beyond that pool of light, a young woman stood beside a rustic wooden chair, a leather traveling case at her feet and a man's clothes draped across her arm.

The traveling case and the garments were Mitchell's; he recognized the items readily enough, but he knew for a fact that he had never seen the woman before. He would have remembered, for she was without a doubt the most beautiful creature he had ever seen!

Her auburn hair was unbound and hung in thick waves down her back, and the figure encased in the gold satin bodice and the gold-and-red patterned skirt was slender and quite temptingly rounded. Her clothing was not unlike that worn by a Gypsy fortune-teller, and around her creamy neck she wore a necklace of thick, gold-painted seashells. Long gold loops hung from her pretty ears, and as she moved, arranging his clothes across the cain seat, the gold loops swung back and forth, touching first the smooth ivory skin of her soft cheek then the equally smooth flesh of her long, graceful neck.

He could not discern the color of her eyes, for they were shadowed, but they were set in a cameo-like face and framed by delicately arched brows. Her lips were full and as tempting as ripe cherries. So tempting, in fact, that Mitchell felt his blood stirring in his veins.

He had to be dreaming! Such women did not come to him in real life.

Just the sight of the ephemeral beauty quickened the beat of his heart, and hoping to savor the experience, perhaps even coax the vision to come to him, he closed his eyes again. After a moment his wish came true, for he sensed the woman standing beside him.

Even in his dreams she smelled of cleanliness and just a light sprinkling of lilac water. When she placed the back of her hand across his brow, as if testing him for fever, he obeyed a very primal impulse by reaching out and catching her around her slender waist. Still with his eyes shut, he pulled her across his chest, slid his free hand around to the nape of her neck, and urged her face down to his so he could claim her lips.

Beneath the flowing Gypsy clothes, her body was unbound by corset or stays, and at the feel of her warm, womanly softness, Mitchell felt the rise of heat inside him—the rebirth of a passion so long dormant he had thought it was lost to him forever. Loath to shatter this welcome sensation, even if it was only a figment of his imagination, he drew the beauty even closer, the weight of her firm, round breasts pressed against his chest. His hands traveled the length of her slender back, and with each new inch discovered, his ignited passion burned hotter and hotter.

Her lips were heaven—soft and heart-stoppingly pliable—and Mitchell sought ecstasy by parting those lips with his tongue, his purpose to deepen the kiss.

Please, God, do not let me wake. Let this dream last a few more minutes!

As he had previously suspected, heaven no longer heard his prayers, for no sooner had he begged for the dream to continue than it ended abruptly.

"Take your hands off me!" the woman said, her breath warm on his face. "Let go of me this instant!"

Chapter Four

"*L*et me go!" she repeated, and this time her angry demand for release was punctuated by an elbow that threatened to bore a hole through Mitchell's solar plexus. He let her go. At the same time his eyelids flew open, and he watched in surprise as the vision pushed away from him and put as much distance between them as was possible in so small a room. The lovely breasts that had so recently reposed against Mitchell's chest now moved up and down as she gulped air into her lungs.

"How dare you!" she said, those once-pliable lips rigid with outrage. "You . . . you libertine!"

The vision was no vision at all, but flesh and blood! Angry flesh and blood. And considering her Gypsy costume, Mitchell felt fortunate that she had not seen fit to put a curse on him. A very real curse from a very real woman.

"I thought you were a dream," he said quietly. "A beautiful dream."

For a moment Delia was tempted to believe him. If she had not known who he was and why he had come to Ems Regis, she might even have smiled and forgiven him. After all, his was the first kiss she had ever actually enjoyed. No, she had more than enjoyed it! Honesty compelled her to admit that much. When he held her pressed against his rock-hard chest, she had

felt a flame ignite inside her—a flame that promised
the sort of passion she had previously only dreamed
about.

During the three years of her betrothal, her fiancé,
Lieutenant Nicholas Zidell, had held her in his arms
many times, but never had his embrace roused even
a spark of emotion inside her. Never had she longed
for Nicholas's kisses to continue. Not so with this
man's kisses. With him, Delia had wanted to—

Heaven help her! She must be insane, for she was
indulging in spinsterish fantasies about a man who
might well wish to do away with a child for standing
between him and his uncle's wealth.

Delia had come to the bedchamber for only one
purpose, to bring the man his clothes and valise. Before she knew what he was about, however, he had
caught her around the waist, holding her captive in an
iron-hard embrace. Without seeming to rush, he had
urged her head down to his so he could capture her
lips. Then he had kissed her.

When his lips touched hers, they had been firm, yet
gentle. Immediately all thought ceased, leaving only
her senses to do battle. Not that they fought very hard.
Not when the warmth of his body against hers sent
tingling sensations skittering down her spine, while the
masculine, sleepy smell of him filled her nostrils in a
dizzying way no champagne could match. Then there
was the taste of him.

With mesmerizing proficiency, he had deepened the
kiss, teasing and coaxing a response from her—a response she had done nothing to discourage. Not at
first. Not until an ounce of sanity somehow fought its
way to her bemused brain, and she remembered that
the man kissing her was Major Mitchell Holcomb.

She had pushed away from him, and now, as she
stood beside the chest of drawers, her hand splayed
on the wooden surface to help her maintain her bal-

ance, she tried to steady her breathing. Tried to pretend his kisses had not had the least effect upon her.

The pretense failed miserably. Her senses were not deceived, nor was the man who stared at her as if he knew her thoughts. Slowly, a smile tugged at the corners of those lips that had so recently hypnotized her lips. With lazy movements, as if he had not a care in the world, he crossed his arms behind his head, the action causing the blanket to fall open to his waist, inviting Delia to notice the remarkable contours of his bare chest.

From the moment she had entered the room, she had been striving valiantly to keep her gaze from straying to his handsome profile. What a jest on her, for now her attention was all but riveted to his muscular arms, his powerful-looking shoulders, and the broad expanse of chest that narrowed to a slim waist, leaving no doubt as to his manliness.

He had to be the most blatantly masculine man Delia had ever seen, and the lock of ink-black hair that fell across his forehead, far from making him appear unkempt, succeeded in giving him an appealingly carefree look. That look was totally misleading, of course, for when the moonlight suddenly shifted toward the bed, revealing his surprisingly gray eyes, the emotion lurking in those orbs was hunger. It was the hunger of a man for a woman, and the realization sent a thrill of warning to every nerve ending in Delia's body.

Beware, her saner self cautioned, *for before you lies certain danger.*

"If you are not, indeed, a figment of my imagination," he said, breaking into her thoughts, "may I be so presumptuous as to ask who you are?"

Delia could not believe her ears. Was he in earnest? Surely he must know who she was. After all, he had come in answer to her letter. "Do you make sport of me, sir?"

He smiled, and suddenly Delia felt breathless. There should be a law against a man having such even, white teeth. As for the slight cleft that teased his chin, that had obviously been a gift from Satan himself.

"As delightful as making sport of you might be, my pretty Gypsy, I assure you I have no idea who you are."

Gypsy? For a moment she had forgotten that she had fled London with only the clothes on her back, and that since her arrival at Sky Cottage she had worn the simple skirts and bodices that had once belonged to her friend Maria.

With a calmness she was far from feeling, Delia returned the major's smile, though she had no hope that her smile would have as devastating an effect upon him as his had had upon her. "It would appear that we have something in common, sir, for I do not know your name. Nor why you are come to Sky Cottage."

"I am Mitchell Holcomb," he said at last, "lately of His Majesty's Army. And I have come from London to speak with a female who calls herself Miss Cordelia Barrington."

Calls herself!

At first Delia took umbrage at his insulting tone, and she might have given him a set-down he would not soon forget had she not begun to realize the significance of his words. He spoke as though he did not even suspect Delia of being the person he sought. If that was true, then perhaps she could keep her identity hidden until she discerned his true purpose in being in Ems Regis—his plans for little Robbie. "Was this person expecting you, sir?"

"This person?" he repeated. "Are you telling me you do not know her?"

Delia lowered her gaze so he could not read the truth in her eyes. "Perhaps if you described her to me."

"I cannot, for I know nothing of her."

"What!" Could he be telling the truth? "Would you have me believe that you traveled all the way from London on what could prove to be a hunt for mares' nest?"

"Well, I, uh—"

"Before you left town, did you not inquire about the woman you seek? Her looks? Her age? Her family?"

He was not smiling now, and Delia heard a muttered swear word, as if he might be embarrassed that he had left such an important task undone. "It was foolish of me, I suppose. But I had other things on my mind. Besides, there was no one to ask."

No one? Then the servants at the town house must have done as she bid them and left London. Good. Their safety had been weighing upon her conscience.

"All I know of the woman," the major said, "is that she claims a certain child was put into her keeping."

Claims? He had a nerve! Casting aspersions on her word, as though she were already convicted of inventing facts to suit her own purposes. Delia pressed her lips together to stay the scathing remarks she longed to utter.

"If what the woman says of the child's identity is true—which I take leave to doubt—then it would be logical to assume she is his nursery maid."

Which he took leave to doubt! Delia's back straightened, a sign the late Lord Sheffield could have informed any interested parties gave evidence of his step-daughter's anger. How dare this . . . this *soldier* question her veracity.

"Or perhaps," he continued, obviously unaware of the insult he had given, "the woman is a governess, since she is educated enough to write a letter. If so, then she is probably some prune-faced spinster in her middle years. More I cannot say."

Prune faced? And in her middle years? This was the outside of enough! Was he trying to provoke her?

"Whoever she may be," he continued, "I wish to ask her some questions."

"About the child?"

"That," he replied, "and about a lady who has gone missing."

"A missing lady? I do not—"

"A Miss Sheffield," he said. "My cousin was murdered in the lady's town house, and since the night of the murder, no one has seen or heard of the lady."

Delia bit her lip to keep herself from speaking. Did he truly believe there were two women? Or could he be dissembling to put her off her guard? There were any number of people in London who could have told him about Lord Sheffield and his lordship's only child—his step-daughter, Cordelia Barrington. True, Delia had not been much in society in the past two years, not since the loss of her fiancé, followed closely by her dear steppapa's illness and untimely demise, but neither had she fallen off the face of the earth. That is, not until the murder.

Had he not thought to ask the neighbors about the occupants of the town house? Or was he being devious, trying to fool her into a false sense of security? Whatever his plan, the desire for self-preservation prompted Delia to keep her identity a secret. At least until she could judge the major's full purpose in coming here.

"You did not tell me your name," he said, breaking into her thoughts.

"It is De—" Biting off the last syllable and calling herself all kinds of fool, she tried to cover her mistake. "You may call me Dee."

"Just Dee? Have you no last name?"

"Eskew," Delia replied, saying the only name that came to mind.

His face registered surprise. "Eskew? Surely you cannot be related to the old woman who—"

"My grandmother," she interrupted, preferring to

voice a lie rather than have him recall the tea Nadja had given him. "She owns this cottage."

"Well, then, Dee Eskew, you must have seen the Barrington woman, for she wrote in her letter that she was staying here. Furthermore, she gave the impression that she had resided here for two months. And what of a Miss Sheffield? She, too, is from London. Have you seen or heard of her?"

Delia shook her head. That, at least, was the truth, for there was no Miss Sheffield; there never had been. Having once read that successful liars kept as close to the truth as possible, Delia said, "Since I arrived at Sky Cottage, sir, there have been only two women here. Nadja Eskew and me."

After returning to her bedchamber and pushing an oak washstand against the door for added security, Delia spent what remained of the night considering what was best to do. Unfortunately, her mental effort was not rewarded with any momentous inspiration, so by daybreak she decided she had but one option. Since she could not take Robbie to his grandfather until the babe and Nadja returned to the cottage, nor could she go back to London for fear of being the assassin's next target, the only logical course was to remain in Ems Regis.

Whatever the major had in mind for the true heir, Delia did not think *she* had anything to fear from him. Not as long as she kept her head and her distance. She certainly meant to do the latter, for a woman with any pretensions to common sense would know better than to get too close to a man with Major Holcomb's handsome face and form, never mind the ability he had already demonstrated for exciting her blood.

"Forget that kiss," she muttered, angry with herself for allowing the memory to edge its way back into her thoughts. "Ignore him. For as long as Major Holcomb remains at the cottage, which should not be many more hours, treat him as though he were an old man of ninety-plus years.''

It was excellent advice, and by the time Nadja's cockerel announced the coming of morning, Delia had convinced herself that ignoring Mitchell Holcomb would not be all that difficult. Of course, that was before she saw him again.

Once she had completed her morning ablutions, Delia tied her loose hair at her nape with a ribbon, donned a dark blue skirt and a cream bodice that had once belonged to Maria, then went belowstairs to see what she could find to break her fast. Of course, with Nadja gone Delia was not at all certain she could put together an edible meal. She could make a decent cup of tea, but beyond that she had no culinary skills. Until now, she had never had the need for such talents, for Lord Sheffield had provided his wife and his stepdaughter with a more than comfortable lifestyle that included servants to see to all their needs.

A pity Delia had never paid attention to how eggs were cooked. Or for that matter, how a simple bowl of porridge was prepared.

Deciding it was a bit late to be lamenting the discrepancies in her education, she opened the entry door to let in the soft morning light and the fresh sea air, then did the same with the rear door that gave access to the small vegetable garden. Later, once she had stoked and built up the fire and there remained no more chores with which she might procrastinate, she took a fortifying breath then investigated the larder built into the corner near the back door.

To her relief, the larder was well stocked. On one shelf she found a covered dish containing goat cheese, and on another a wooden cutting board bearing a crusty loaf of hearty brown bread that had been baked only two days ago then wrapped in a clean cloth to protect it.

She smiled when she discovered a crockery marmalade pot that held some of Nadja's delicious apple butter. With such a treat, even bread and cheese would seem a feast. And no cooking necessary. A circumstance for which she and Major Holcomb should thank their guardian angels.

After setting two places at the much-scoured deal table, Delia filled the teapot, set a quilted cozy over it to allow the tea to steep, then took the bread to the table, where she could slice it without making too much of a mess. The knife had only just penetrated the topmost crust when she heard the door to one of the two guest bedchambers open.

The major was a large man, but his booted feet made very little sound on the wooden stairs; far less noise than the overloud beating of Delia's heart. Silently she called herself an entire string of derogatory epithets for reacting like the veriest ninnyhammer simply because a man was in the house. Though in truth, he was not just any man, but the man who had kissed her and stirred emotions inside her she had not known existed.

Trying for some semblance of normalcy, she pasted a smile upon her face, then turned to greet him. "Good morning, Major. My breakfast is simple, but you are welcome to join—"

At first sight of him, both the words and the smile deserted her. His clothes, though a bit the worse for having been rain soaked then dried before the fire, fit him to perfection and were a vast improvement over the humble quilt he had worn the evening before. The Devonshire brown coat and striped waistcoat were beautifully cut and adhered to his shoulders and chest without a single wrinkle, while the skintight fawn breeches revealed muscular thighs that bunched and relaxed with each successive step descended. The effect was so mesmerizing that for the life of her, Delia could not look away.

His top boots showed signs of yesterday's rain, and his cheeks and chin were shadowed with whiskers only slightly lighter in color than the blue-black of the hair on his head. Still, he was every inch the soldier, and he held himself straight and tall. Apparently not the least bit self-conscious about his appearance, he approached her with such confidence it made Delia's breath catch in her throat.

She numbered among her town acquaintances several Corinthians and at least that many gentlemen of the dandy set, and she knew without question that half those men—not to mention every last coxcomb in London—would even now be attempting to emulate Mitchell Holcomb's attire and bearing. Attempting, but not succeeding.

"Good day to you, ma'am," he said in reply to her previous greeting.

Though she had not finished her invitation for him to join her, he strode to the table where she stood slicing the bread. Sawing through it might be a better description, for she was unaccountably nervous at the thought of breaking her fast with such an elegant and undeniably masculine gentleman.

As often happened when she was nervous, she began to whistle softly. Whistling was her only musical talent, and she did it well. Though her choice of song had been without malice, it was a ditty from the previous century called "A Tulip on the Strut." It had been one of her stepfather's favorites, for it ridiculed an empty-headed dandy in powder and patch whose only love was the cut of his coat.

"So," the major said, a smile pulling at the corners of his expressive mouth, "am I to assume from your song that you think me a coxcomb? Not very flattering, I must say."

Doubly mortified now, she stammered, "You . . . you are familiar with that song?"

"Quite. It may interest you to know that when a

battle is imminent, some soldiers resort to silence to calm their nerves, while others sing songs from their childhood. I do not think I have ever engaged in a battle that was not preceded by at least half a dozen choruses of 'A Tulip on the Strut.' "

Delia's face felt hotter than the teapot beneath the cozy. Why had she chosen that, of all songs? He would think she was mocking him.

He looked at her then, one eyebrow raised, as if in question. "Are we about to do battle, Miss Eskew?"

"I hope not," she said, giving her full attention to the further mutilation of the crusty loaf, "for I am not at my best in the early hours."

After a silence that seemed to go on forever, Mitchell slid the ladder-back chair from beneath the deal table and settled himself as comfortably as possible. "Did you know," he began, "that in olden times, a woman who whistled was deemed to be possessed by the devil?"

"What!"

At least she had put down the knife and was looking at him now. Last night Mitchell had been unable to determine the color of her eyes, but now he saw that they were a lovely topaz color, with the center of the iris a golden hue and the outer rim of the circle almost brown.

"I do not believe you," she said.

"Oh my honor, ma'am, it is true."

To keep from getting lost in those topaz eyes, he continued with his story. "As I recall, should said whistling female be so careless as to purse her lips and blow within hearing of the milch cows, the milk inside the bovines was guaranteed to dry up. At which time, the whistler's father or her husband, or some other good and just man of the family, was expected to procure a sturdy stick—one no thicker than his thumb, mind you—for the purpose of beating the devil out of the woman."

Mitchell had hoped the foolish story would put his Gypsy enchantress at her ease. It did not. And when her lovely lips—lips whose softness he remembered all too well—showed not the least inclination to smile, he decided she had been in earnest when she said she was not at her best in the morning.

After another silence, he motioned toward the bread and cheese. "That looks delicious. As does the apple butter." He sniffed the air. "And I believe I smell tea. Though it is Bohea, I think, and not that rather exotic blend Nadja Eskew gave me last evening."

He had meant to ask her about the strangely soporific powers of the tea given him by the Gypsy, and he would have done so if the young woman's cheeks had not suddenly turned as pink as the roses in his mother's garden at Fernbourne House. Surprised by her apparent embarrassment, he allowed the subject of Nadja's tea to go unaddressed for the moment.

"This is Bohea," Dee Eskew said rather stiffly. After setting aside the knife she had been using, she reached for the teapot. "Shall I pour you a cup?"

"Please," he replied.

Mitchell had thought the bread and cheese looked delicious, but as he watched the young woman remove the quilted cozy, then bend forward to pour him a cup of the pungent brew, her thick eyelashes resting against her silky cheeks, he decided she looked far more delicious than the repast. The ladies of London, in their expensive silks and satins, could take a lesson from the Gypsies—or at least one Gypsy. With her unpretentious bodice and skirt and her long, thick hair tied back with a ribbon, Dee Eskew was the most appealing woman Mitchell had ever met.

While she poured, he studied her hands. They were slender and elegantly shaped, and to his surprise the skin was satiny smooth. Pampered hands, he thought, not at all what one would expect to discover on a person who presumably was no stranger to physical labor. Come to think of it, her entire complexion was lighter than that of her Gypsy grandmother. Several shades lighter.

And, of course, there was the matter of her refined speech. He had been too distracted last evening to notice anything other than her beauty. Not surprising, considering the combined effects of tasting those tempting lips and drinking that deuced suspicious tea.

"Damnation," he muttered.

At some point he had obviously lost the finely honed intuitiveness that had saved his life many a time in the past nine years. Otherwise, he would have noticed earlier that there were no familial similarities between the short, dark-eyed Nadja Eskew and the tall, topaz-eyed young woman who stood before him. But why the charade?

Busy pondering that question and cursing himself for being a fool, he did not notice that Dee Eskew had grown unexplainably quiet. In fact, the first inkling he had of impending disaster came when she suddenly gasped and dropped the teapot, spilling steaming liquid all over the table.

In his attempt to avoid having scalding tea land in his lap, Mitchell jumped back, knocking over his chair. While he scrambled to his feet, he realized the cause of his hostess's distress. A man—roughly dressed and resembling a mountain on two legs—stood in the open doorway. Before Mitchell could turn and challenge the fellow for his ill manners in entering the cottage without first making his presence known, the mountain rushed toward him, growling and brandishing a leather-covered cudgel.

Still unbalanced from his attempt to escape the hot tea, Mitchell was at the man's mercy. Hoping to deflect the blow that was clearly intended for his head, Mitchell pivoted to his right, managing to swing his upper body aside a few inches before the cudgel came down. Unfortunately, he did not escape harm entirely, for the blow landed with considerable force on the side of his neck.

Immediately, the room began to spin and colored spots danced before his eyes. Though he grabbed at the edge of the table in hopes of maintaining his balance, he felt himself losing control. The table was sturdy, but pitted against Mitchell's weight, it lost the battle and began to move forward, the legs making a loud scraping noise as they scraped across the brick floor. Denied the support of the table, Mitchell felt himself falling to the floor.

The last thing he remembered was the sound of Dee Eskew's ear-shattering scream.

Chapter Five

*D*elia swallowed the second scream that clamored to escape her throat. The last thing she needed was to give way to hysteria, and she was already too close to that deplorable state to allow another scream to put her even a hair's breadth closer. Alone with a cudgel-wielding brute, she knew if she surrendered her mental strength she lost all hope of survival. The major was down, and sensing that it would do her no good to beg for mercy from his vicious attacker, she bit down on her lower lip to help her remain silent.

While the man was occupied kicking the fallen Major Holcomb in the ribs, to make certain he was not faking his loss of consciousness, Delia moved her hand as unobtrusively as possible and snatched the knife she had used to slice the bread, hiding the blade in the folds of her full skirt. Slowly, she backed away from the table, not stopping until her spine collided with the larder door.

Considering her reasons for fleeing London, any intruder would have frightened her, but the size and fierceness of the man in the leather waistcoat and rough workman's breeches filled her with terror. She stared at him, she could do nothing else, for if she dared blink her eyes she feared he would be on her in that instant, dispatching her as he had dispatched Major Holcomb.

The major was a large man—tall and remarkably
fit—but this fellow was huge. Fully six and a half feet
tall, and weighing at least seventeen stone, he was a
giant; one who compounded the degree of his intimidation by possessing a mean, angry-looking face only
a mother could love. If, indeed, such a man had ever
had a mother.

"Fetch the Lunnon lady," he ordered, erasing any
doubts Delia may have had that he had come for her.

"Wh . . . who?" she asked, fear all but closing her
throat.

"The lady what come 'ere from Lunnon. Fetch 'er.
And be quick about it," he added, brandishing the
cudgel in case she had missed seeing him use it to
knock Major Holcomb to the floor, "unless ye want a
taste of this."

"No, no. I do not."

"Then don't keep me waiting. I've come a long way,
I 'ave, and I've business wif the lady."

Stalling, trying to gauge how far she was from the
rear door without actually turning to look at it, Delia
said, "What sort of business?"

"As to that, reckon the Lunnon lady will know
the answer."

Delia knew all right. No one had to tell her that
this brute of a man had been sent to silence her. He
was not the person she had seen shoot and kill William Holcomb, but he possessed the same sort of cold,
uncaring eyes.

For the better part of eight weeks Delia had been
peering over her shoulder, living in almost constant
dread of just such a visitor. Even so, she had not realized she would be quite so terrified when the assassin
finally arrived. Her knees shook like a blancmange,
and beads of perspiration ran down her nape and over
her shoulders to disappear inside the rounded neck of
her bodice. All that allowed her to remain standing

was the knowledge that the man did not know she was Cordelia Barrington.

Pretending a bravado she was far from feeling, she said, "What makes you think the lady you seek is here?"

"She be 'ere, right enough. We been looking all over Lunnon, wif nofing to show for our troubles 'cept cold trails. Then," he added, motioning toward the recumbent major, "the toff there gives us our first clue."

"The major?" The question slipped out before Delia could stop it. Reason told her that he could not be linked with this fellow, else he would not now be lying unconscious in the floor. Still—

" 'E started nosing around," the man continued, as if pleased to have an audience to whom he could brag of his ingenuity. "Been offering gelt for information about the murder of 'is cousin. The murder what was done in the Lunnon lady's 'ouse."

Delia stole a glance at the poor major, who lay as still as death. If he had been offering money for information, surely that proved he had not had anything to do with his cousin's death.

The giant had continued to speak, and Delia had to force her attention back to his words. "That's when we started trailing the gent close-like. Figured 'is money would open some mummers before long, and 'e would find the lady for us. And so 'e did."

Delia's breath caught in her throat. The major had led this terrifying man to her. He might not have meant to, since he had come in answer to her letter to his uncle, but the result was the same. He had come, and so had this villain. And now the major was lying on the floor, dead for all she knew, while she remained to face who knew what ordeal.

". . . and when the toff suddenly left town, that's when 'is lordship told us to follow."

What was the lout saying? *His lordship?* Had she heard him correctly? Surely this cutthroat was not employed by a peer.

" 'Course we lost 'im there for a time, on account of we went all the way to Ems Regis. But a fisher lad there told us 'e'd directed some swell in a curricle and pair to this 'ere cottage. And now we be 'ere."

Obviously finished with his story, he glanced around the room, as if expecting to see the "Lunnon lady" standing in the corner, just waiting to be discovered. When she did not miraculously appear, he snapped at Delia to shake a leg. "Time's wasting. Fetch the lady. We ain't got all day."

Delia, realizing that the man had said "we" several times, resisted the urge to look over her shoulder, afraid she would discover the other half of the pair just waiting to pounce. Thankfully, no one grabbed her from behind, but she still trembled at the thought that there might be another villain outside somewhere, perhaps the same man who shot William Holcomb.

Though she wished with all her heart that there was someone to help her—some knight in shining armor coming that very moment to whisk her out of harm's way—her mind told her unequivocally that there was no such rescuer. Logic told her that if there was any rescuing to be done, she would have to do it. She knew as well that if she waited too long to do something constructive, any opportunity to save herself would be lost.

Telling herself that it was now or never, she raised the knife in what she hoped was a threatening manner. "Get out of here," she said. "There is no one in the cottage but me and that poor gentleman on the floor, and upon my oath I will use this weapon if you do not leave immediately."

The giant merely laughed. "Oooh, a little Gypsy 'ellcat. I'm that afeared, I am."

As if to underscore his lack of concern for her and

her weapon, the man stepped around the major's outstretched legs and began to walk toward her, his ugly mouth set in a leer. "If the Lunnon lady b'aint 'ere, mayhap we'll 'ave us a bit of fun while we wait. A quick shag for me troubles. What say ye, girlie? Ye lift yer skirts sweet-like, and mayhap ole Georgie'll forget 'e ever clamped 'is peepers on ye. Be a shame to kill such a pretty wench."

He was now so close to her that Delia smelled the onions and stale ale that clung to his clothes and his lank, oily hair. Quicker than she had thought possible in a man so large, he reached out and grabbed her, his ham-like hand closing around her wrist and shaking it until the knife fell to the floor with an impotent clink.

"Now, then," he said, his dirty fingers closing around her neck and yanking her roughly toward him, "give us a kiss, there's a good girl, and I'll—"

He got no further, for as if by magic, one of Nadja's ladder-back chairs suddenly came down on his head, exploding into dozens of pieces. For a moment, the loutish face registered shock, then without another sound the man fell against Delia, grabbing at her shoulders, his weight pulling her down with him. She tried to break free of his grasp, but he was just too strong, and when they finally landed, his massive upper torso was sprawled across hers, knocking the air from her lungs and pinning her to the rough brick floor.

For just an instant she thought she might smother.

Though not certain which motivated her most, disgust or fear, Delia pushed and squirmed until she dislodged the villain a few inches, at least enough to allow her to draw in a ragged breath. "Get him off me!" she screamed at last. "Get him off!"

Mitchell dragged himself to his feet then grabbed the chair he had once occupied, but when he lifted it on high, his intention to crash it against the giant's thick skull, blinding pain exploded inside his own brain. At the same time, nausea threatened to distract him from his purpose. Afraid he possessed only enough strength for one blow, he willed the sickness away. Focusing all his resolve and every ounce of his energy on the task at hand, he swung, bringing the furniture down with all the power left in him.

Fortunately, he hit the man solidly, and the giant went down like a felled tree. Unfortunately, he took poor Dee Eskew with him.

She was understandably frightened, and while she lay on the floor pinned beneath the man, she kept yelling something. Mitchell was not certain what she yelled, for his ears still buzzed from the force of the cudgel blow to his neck. Still, he marshaled his strength sufficiently to bend down, grab the sprawling giant by his leather vest, and pull him aside enough for Dee to squirm free.

While Mitchell willed the room to stop tilting noticeably to the right and the walls to stop their blasted weaving and twisting, Dee rolled onto her side, gasping for breath. Since he was having trouble with his own breathing, he let her remain there until she had regained her strength. By the time she pushed herself upright and rose to her feet, he, too, had reclaimed a semblance of normalcy.

She came to him at once. "I thought you were dead," she said, her voice understandably shaky. "Thank heaven that you are not, for I . . . I feared I was all alone."

"Madam, your concern for my welfare quite overwhelms me."

Her cheeks went bright pink. "Sir! I did not mean it the way it came out! Naturally, I was concerned for your—"

"Please," he said, "do not give it another thought. As it happens, I am not that easy to insult. And even less easy to kill. Others have tried."

"I am delighted to hear it." Immediately, the pink

in her cheeks turned quite crimson. "I did not mean I was happy that others had made attempts upon your life, sir, but that you have survived them."

Now thoroughly embarrassed, she waved her hand as if to put an end to the conversation. "For the sake of expediency, Major, pray, let us leave the discussion of your enemies—as well as my speech of gratitude— for some later time. At the moment, we have more important matters to discuss." She glanced uneasily toward the fellow lying on the ground. "Though the very idea makes me sick to my stomach, I have reason to believe there may be two malefactors."

Mitchell looked quickly at both doors, thankful to find them empty.

As if suspecting him of doubting her word, Dee squared her shoulders, her chin jutting out a bit pugnaciously. "The man said 'we' more than once."

"You are certain?"

"Quite. And if there lurks outside somewhere another brute like the one on the floor, I feel it imperative that we leave here as quickly as possible."

Mitchell was in full agreement. Two facts convinced him that discretion was, indeed, the better part of valor. First, the giant who lay unconscious at their feet would not remain immobile much longer, and when he recovered he would be spoiling for revenge. And second, at the moment Mitchell did not have the strength to subdue a newborn kitten, never mind a loutish fellow bent on retaliation.

"I do not know where the other man may be," Dee said, breaking into his thoughts, "but wherever he is, we must not meet him."

"What do these men want? Do you know?"

That deep blush was in evidence again, though why it should be so, Mitchell could not even guess.

"I never saw the giant before today," she said. "If he is to be believed, however, he and his accomplice followed you from town."

"Me? Whatever for?"

She hesitated, and for a moment Mitchell thought she meant not to reply. Finally she said, "Whatever their reasons, we must go, Major, for I am persuaded that they, along with their leader, will be satisfied with nothing less than our lives."

"Their leader?"

"Someone the lout referred to as 'his lordship.'"

While Mitchell considered that piece of information, Dee Eskew stepped over to the back door and peered outside, being careful not to reveal her presence. "There is someone in the stable," she whispered, as though a man who had remained outside during all manner of screaming and furniture splitting would suddenly come running at the sound of normal conversation.

It was proof of Mitchell's still befogged brain that he very nearly laughed, and he might have done so had he not caught himself in time. "Most likely the accomplice is keeping their horses out of sight so no one passing in the lane will grow suspicious and stop to investigate."

As she had done, he walked to the rear door, then peered around the corner. The stable door was ajar, and someone was inside; there was no question about that, for the man's presence was upsetting the high-strung grays. Even at a distance, Mitchell could hear frightened neighing and the nervous pounding of hooves on the hard-packed earth floor. "Stay here," he said. "I will return directly."

Accustomed to strict obedience from the soldiers under his command, he expected her to comply with his orders. In this assumption he erred, for as he stepped outside, skirted around the muddy vegetable garden, then crept toward the stable, she followed right behind him.

Knowing there was no time to waste in argument, he motioned her around to his left and pointed to the foot-long wooden dowel that was used to secure the door. The peg hung from a rope fastened to the door frame, and the moment she had the peg in hand, Mitchell slammed his entire body against the stable door, holding it shut while she slid the dowel through the two iron rings that served as a lock.

"Hey!" a man yelled from inside the stable. "What's the idea? Georgie, is that you out there? This b'aint no time for foolery. Let me out. Georgie?"

Seconds later, the accomplice began to push from the other side of the door, and judging by the force of the onslaught, the wooden peg would not hold for very long. "Come," Dee Eskew said, grabbing hold of Mitchell's hand and pulling him behind her. "I know a place where we can hide."

After nine years of military service, a good deal of those years spent in enemy-held territory, Mitchell had learned the value of knowing when to stay and when to go. This was definitely the time to go, so he let her lead him past the stable and away from the cottage.

They ran for the first few minutes, startling a pair of red squirrels who skittered up a birch tree with all haste, and alarming songbirds to desert their perches and take flight. The ground was rough and still damp from yesterday's heavy rain, and when Mitchell could detect no sound of footfalls behind them, he insisted they slow to a brisk walk. "Breaking a leg will serve no good purpose."

"But—"

"Besides," he added when she appeared about to argue, "we will make less noise if we walk. Personally, I see no point in assisting our pursuers to follow us."

"You are right," she said, her breath labored from the exertion. "I was not thinking."

"Of course you were not." An unholy light came into his gray eyes. "It has long been my belief that thinking should be left to those who do it best. In short, to us males."

"Of all the conceited, arrogant—" Delia bit back the remainder of her retort. From the way the major's lips twitched at the corners, as if he was trying not to smile, she realized he was merely attempting to ease the tension that had her insides tied in a knot. The plan might have worked, too, had she not been far too frightened for jocularity. For now, motivated by a strong desire for self-preservation, she turned and began to walk at a brisk pace.

She lead them inland toward the Downs, past a stand of centuries-old yews and later a pair of tall, impressive, silver-barked beech trees. Not that she had the time or the inclination to notice the beauty of her surroundings. She was far too intent on reaching their ultimate destination, which was a hill fort constructed even before the Roman invasion, some two thousand or more years ago. She had been to the fort several times since coming to Ems Regis, for the place had some special meaning for Nadja, who liked to go there to commune with nature.

Delia had enjoyed accompanying the old Gypsy to the ancient site. Traveling the three miles had offered her an opportunity to stretch her limbs and to get a breath of fresh air. Now, however, she walked those miles because she hoped to put as much distance as possible between her and the men who wished to silence her forever.

Forever silent. Just giving thought to the words made her tremble. She wanted to live. Until a few minutes ago, she had not realized just how desperately she wanted it. She was twenty-eight years old, and though some might call her past praying for, she had done none of the things she had dreamed of doing with her life.

For one thing, she had always thought she would marry one day. As a result of the handsome dowry set aside for her by her stepfather, there were still a number of gentlemen of the *ton* willing to offer her their hand in marriage. Unfortunately, Delia did not want that sort of arrangement. She wanted a love match.

No longer in her first blush of youth—or even her second, for that matter—she realized the chances were not good that she would ever find someone whose heart and mind marched with hers. Still, that was what she dreamed of, someone whose soul was in step with her soul.

She longed to know the joy of loving and being loved in return. Not just settling for the comfort of a home and family, but real love.

She wanted the grand passion!

She had been betrothed, of course. She had accepted Nicholas Zidell's ring during her second London Season, but as the years of her betrothal to the lieutenant dragged on, and she could not bring herself to set the date for the wedding, she had been obliged to face the fact that she did not love him.

She liked him. She admired him. At first, she had even been infatuated with him—or perhaps she had merely been infatuated with his smart blue naval uniform—but she had never truly loved him. Not as he deserved to be loved, and certainly not as she wished to love.

Naturally, she had grieved when Nicholas was killed at Trafalgar. He was a kind and compassionate human being, one whose death was a tragic loss. And yet, honesty compelled her to admit that she was not sorry to be freed from their engagement, and not a little relieved to be spared a future as Mrs. Zidell.

"Is that our destination?" the major said, bringing her thoughts back to the present. "That rampart?"

"It is, sir."

Perhaps eighty yards or so in the distance stood a broad embankment that rose about fifteen feet into the air. The decaying wall-like ridge was composed of earth, debris, and chalk rock fragments, with the chalk accounting for what looked like white lumpy dots. According to what Nadja had told Delia, the rampart, which had been built before the time of Christ, circled roughly sixty acres of land and contained hundreds of little walled areas.

"On the other side of the rampart is a hill fort," Delia said. "I thought we might hide there."

"And the moat?" he asked, pointing to the trench immediately in front of the rampart. "Does it circle the wall completely?"

At Delia's nod, he stepped to the edge and looked down the nearly vertical sides. "This is purely a guess, madam, but I would say this little ditch is at least fifteen feet deep and twice that wide. Personally, I cannot jump thirty feet. Can you?"

"Of course I cannot," she replied.

"Never tell me you expect us to climb down this side then back up the other, for I—"

"Certainly not. Nor would I try anything so foolish, for I do not cherish the idea of multiple broken bones. In addition to the steepness, the ground is heavily pocked with bumps and hollows that are just waiting to trip the unwary."

"Courtesy, no doubt, of the prehistoric inhabitants of this area who mined for flint."

"As to that, Major, I fear my knowledge of local history is limited. All I know for certain is that even if it were safe to cross the moat on foot, I could not do so, not after yesterday's heavy rains."

"The reason being," he said, smiling as if to show he was teasing, "that you are made of sugar and will melt if dunked in a little water."

The remark was so ridiculous that Delia was obliged to return his smile. "I might survive a *little* water. Unfortunately, I suspect the moat contains several feet of run-off, and I cannot swim."

"Then how do you propose we get to the safety of the fort?"

"Around to the south there is a narrow footbridge. I cannot tell you who put it there, except that it was not the ancient builders of the fort. Even so, the bridge is old and rather un—"

"Shh," he said. "I hear something."

They stood quietly, not daring to breathe, and while they strained their ears to listen, the serenity of the Downs was broken by the rhythmic thudding of hoof-beats. From the sound of it, there were two horses, and the riders were advancing at a fast pace, making no effort to conceal their approach. Why should they when they had all the advantages on their side?

They were the hunters, on horseback and possibly armed, while their prey were on foot, not a little winded from running and without weapons of any kind. And in Delia's instance at least, frightened almost beyond endurance, for from the sound of it the riders would be bearing down on them at any moment.

As if suddenly charged with energy, the major grabbed her hand and began to run, his direction southerly. Delia was in pretty good physical condition, but the major was running much too fast, pulling her along behind him and not allowing her to slow. They had not gone far when her legs began to cramp from the unaccustomed activity, and her lungs burned with the effort to fill them with sufficient breath. Still, the major gave her no choice but to continue.

She stumbled once and would have fallen if he had not yanked her up. "Come on," he said, "you can do it. I see the bridge up ahead, not more than twenty feet away."

Delia saw it, too. Unfortunately, she had a stitch in her side that ached as though she had been run through by a Roman legionnaire's spear. She was about to insist that they stop for a few moments when she heard the shout behind them.

"There they be, Georgie! Let's get 'em!"

Since the shout was followed by the loud report of

a pistol, with Delia fancying the bullet missed her head by mere inches, the stitch in her side was instantly forgotten. At the sound of the second shot, she discovered just how fast a person could run if sufficiently motivated.

She had never crossed the footbridge before. And for good reason. The design was simple—nothing more than a series of three-foot-long planks, threaded through a weblike weaving of ropes, with the ends of the ropes secured by iron spikes driven into the ground on either side of the moat. The board-and-rope construction alone was enough to deter any sane person from crossing; the fact that the entire expanse swung freely in the air merely added to its undesirability.

There was no knowing the age of the footbridge, but the untreated wood was in an advanced stage of decay, and in places boards were missing entirely. Even so, the major led Delia across the swinging bridge at a reckless speed. With her hand still held firmly in his, she had no recourse but to follow him, all the while holding her breath and praying that she would not stumble or put a foot through a rotted board.

Her prayers must have been heard, for she and the major made it across the quivering span without mishap. To her surprise, once they touched solid ground, he sent her on ahead through the opening in the scarred and pitted earthwork where a wooden gate had once guarded the entrance.

"I will be along directly," he shouted, his breath, like hers, ragged from their run.

Delia did not stop to ask his reason for remaining behind, nor did she pause until she was well and truly hidden behind an angled inner wall that was almost completely obscured by a century's worth of brambles. From where she hid, she could not see the major, nor even guess what he had in mind, but from the loud thumping, it sounded for all the world as if he were kicking something.

To Delia's horror, another pair of shots rang out, and while she clamped her hand over her mouth to keep from crying out, the thumping stopped. Immediately, there was a clattering of boards hitting against one another, then a sudden loud crash, as if the entire bridge had hit the ground. There was also a resounding splash in the muddy water below.

The noise lasted less than a minute, and in the quietness that followed, Delia did not dare breathe. With her heart beating madly inside her chest, she listened for the major.

Where was he? Had he been shot? Had he fallen into the water? Had it been his dead body that made the ominous splashing noise?

After an eternity of silence, Delia heard the sound of boots squishing on the still-damp ground. "Dee," the major called softly. "Where are you?"

He was alive!

Unbelievable relief surged through her, and it was all she could do not to run to him and fling herself upon his broad chest. Instead, she stepped quietly from behind the brambles so he could see her. "Here I am," she replied.

Inside the fort, the mounded land had lain undisturbed for millennia, and every inch of ground was covered by thick weeds, wild herbs, and sharp, spiny gorse. The soft yellow of the gorse was dotted here and there by the lilac-blue of early scabious, and while Delia watched the major come toward her, crushing both shrub and herb beneath his boots, she noticed that he limped slightly, favoring his left leg.

"You are injured," she said, once he reached her. "I heard the pistol. Were you shot? There was a splash, and I thought, I feared—"

"The splash was nothing more serious than a few boards hitting the water. I was not shot, nor in any danger of being so. Fortunately for us, Georgie is a poor marksman, and his efforts are a decided waste of good gunpowder. As for my injury, I used my leg for a mallet, kicking loose the iron spikes that held the ropes of the footbridge in place."

"You did what?"

"Naturally, I would have preferred a hammer or some other tool. But with no such implements at hand, I made do with what I had."

Delia must have looked as stunned as she felt, for he hurried to explain himself. "I had to encourage the footbridge to surrender its already tenuous hold on the earth. I could think of no other way to insure that our pursuers did not cross as we had."

He smiled at her then. "You will be pleased to know that the footbridge hangs from the far side of the moat like some derelict ladder. Utterly useless. A bridge no longer. There is now no way those two would-be murderers can reach us."

When Dee Eskew merely stared at him, as though she could not believe her ears, Mitchell felt a momentary irritation. He did not expect congratulations; after all, he had done only what he thought best to insure their safety, but surely she could muster just a bit of appreciation. "You are very quiet, madam. One might be forgiven for thinking you were not pleased to know those louts had been out-maneuvered."

"To the contrary, sir. I am inordinately pleased to know that we have made good our escape from those two. I was, however, wondering about something else."

"And that would be?" he asked, not hiding the annoyance he felt.

"I was merely wondering, since that was the only existing bridge, how you and I are ever to escape this fort?"

Mitchell could not believe his ears. "Madam, you never told me that was the only bridge!"

"Sir, you never asked!"

Chapter Six

*F*or the past hour, they had done nothing but glare at one another, each apparently waiting for the other to admit culpability for the fact that they had fled the enemy, only to find themselves trapped on what was basically an island. An island without food, water, or shelter.

"Damnation!" the major said at last. "Miss Cordelia Barrington has much to answer for."

Delia was taken aback by his vehemence. Had he somehow guessed her identity? Had she given herself away? Certain she had not done so, she braved it out. "What has Miss Barrington to say to the matter?"

"Plenty. Were it not for that woman's letter, I would not be here. Ergo, I would not have become embroiled in this debacle."

"I hardly think that is *her* fault! After all, the letter was not actually addressed to you."

He muttered something she did not hear, nor wish to. "Madam, you miss the point entirely. Because of a single missive, I am now the target of two louts whose purpose I cannot even guess. Why, I faced Boney's army with less cataclysmic results."

Delia was relieved to know that he had not actually guessed that *she* was Cordelia Barrington; otherwise, she would have reminded him that it was one of Napoleon's men who had wounded him in the side, very

nearly killing him. This time, at least, he was unharmed—or nearly unharmed, if one discounted the
episode with the cudgel. And the bullets had both
missed him entirely! As for the sore foot, that was
most certainly his own fault, and she would refresh
his memory on that point if he persisted in blaming
the letter for all his troubles.

She was still biting her tongue to curb a cutting
retort when a drop of rain landed on the tip of her
nose. Fortunately for the major, the unwanted moisture instantly dissolved all desire on Delia's part to
continue their argument.

Rain! It wanted only that! And her without a bonnet
or a wrap of any kind.

Using the back of her hand, she hastily brushed
away the droplet, then mouthed an inaudible prayer
that the black clouds would keep moving until they
were at least fifty miles away.

Apparently, Major Holcomb did not notice the first
drop, or even the second and third. He had decided
to scale the thick rampart once again, to spy on their
pursuers, and no amount of discussion on Delia's part
would sway him from his intention. She was dis-
covering that he was quite single-minded when there
was a task at hand.

With an agility she could not help but admire, he
climbed the fifteen-foot wall, finding toeholds and fin-
gerholds where none appeared to her. Once at the top
of the rough parapet, he stretched out flat on his stomach, watching and listening quietly in hopes of over-
hearing what the two scoundrels meant to try next.

Earlier, Georgie and his accomplice had circled the
fort—one riding east, the other riding west—looking
for a way across the moat. Naturally, they had not
found any access, so they had met back at the beginning point, both cursing their luck, and not caring a
fig if they were overheard.

"We been bubbled but good, Georgie. There b'aint no way to get to 'em."

"The good part," Georgie replied, "is that there b'aint no way for them to escape."

"There'll be no *good* part about it if 'is lordship finds out there be two more witnesses, and we still ain't finished the job."

"We'll finish it right enough."

"But times awasting. We only got five more days 'til the ball."

"Stubble it!," Georgie said, "and let a man think." He dismounted, then handed his horse's rein to his partner. "Go back there by that tree and tie the cattle. Meanwhile, I'll wait 'ere, patient like, 'til the toff tries summit foolish."

"And what if 'e don't?"

" 'E will. Their morning meal lies on the floor back there at the cottage. Shouldn't be too long 'til they get 'ungry, and when a bloke's innards starts to growling, 'e gets careless."

"Then what?"

Georgie lifted his pistol and aimed at a spot across the moat. "The moment the toff shows his 'ead, *bang*, I'll be waiting. Once 'e's dead, we'll find some way to get that Gypsy gal, then we'll ride back to the cottage and finish off the Lunnon lady."

After the major told Delia what had passed between the two villains, she had not dared show her head, content to remain hidden behind the thick rampart. Not so her fellow exile, who was cut from a different cloth. Apparently he was incapable of remaining motionless, or of waiting for others to initiate the action. For that reason, he climbed the wall once again to see what was happening.

While Mitchell lay there on the parapet, the first few raindrops fell on his head, allowing the water to trickle down past his ears and cheeks, chilling him in the increasingly brisk wind. Earlier he had noticed the amassing of the clouds and the darkening of the sky, and he had hoped the rain would arrive soon. Rain would be good; a storm even better.

If he and Dee Eskew were to escape this cursed trap, they would need something to distract the two louts who watched from the other side of the moat. Since neither man appeared particularly needle-witted, bad weather might be enough to tax their ability to improvise, and with any luck, they might abandon their vigil. "At least," Mitchell muttered, "let us hope so."

In truth, there was no "us," for he was alone on the rampart. Dee sat on the ground just below him, her back to the rough wall, her legs hugged against her, and her head resting on her knees. She was frightened—and with just cause—and Mitchell would have understood if she had given way to tears or even hysteria. To his relief, she had managed thus far to control her fear, doing no more than hug herself, stare at him with wide, questioning eyes, and whistle an undetectable tune beneath her breath.

She would do more than whistle, however, when he told her his plan. Especially since she had already confessed that she could not swim.

She would need his help, and recalling how only yesterday he had envied the birds their freedom, Mitchell did not want to be needed. He wanted a peaceful, uneventful life, with no attachments and no one depending on him.

While he pondered just how needy she might be, his hopes for severe weather were realized and the sky opened up, transforming what had once been a scattering of drops into full-fledged rain. As it had done the day before, the rain soon became a downpour, with ever-increasing amounts of water cascading down the sides of the moat and adding to the depth of what was already there. Visibility was limited, but

Mitchell could see enough to know when the two thugs began to argue about giving up trying to shelter beneath the lone tree.

"But 'is lordship'll say we should've stayed."

Georgie uttered a string of vulgarities. " 'Is lordship b'aint 'ere, freezing 'is arse off and risking the ague. It's you and me as is getting wet and cold, and I'm for a warm fire and a tankard of ale. We can come back later. Not to worry, them two b'aint going no place."

The accomplice was still cursing and grumbling when Georgie rode away, but even before the giant was out of sight, the other man jumped on his horse and hurried after him. "Wait up!" he yelled. "I b'aint waiting 'ere alone."

This was the opportunity Mitchell had been waiting for, and since experience told him that such chances did not come often, nor last long, he knew he must act quickly. More or less sliding down the side of the rampart, he landed mere inches from where Dee sat. "Come," he said, holding out his hand to her, "the men are gone, and we are leaving."

"What?"

"Get up," he said more firmly. "Heaven must love one of us—I daresay it is you, because my life has been far from exemplary. At any rate, we have been given an opportunity to leave this place alive. However, we must act immediately, while we can."

As he had predicted earlier, she merely stared at him, confusion written plainly on her face. Still, she took his outstretched hand and let him pull her to her feet. She was wet through, with her clothes clinging to her body like a second skin, and though she shivered from the cold, she voiced no complaint.

"How . . . how do we leave?" she asked through chattering teeth.

Mitchell thought it best not to answer that question. Instead, he caught both her hands and pulled her close so he could whisper in her ear. "I have been in worse situations than this, Dee, and as you can see, I have lived to tell the tale. Now, I need to know only one thing from you. Will you trust me to get us out of this dilemma?"

At her nod, he continued. "I have a plan, and it is completely workable, but for it to succeed, you must promise to obey me. You must do exactly what I tell you to do, and you must do it without hesitation. Can you make such a promise? If not, tell me now, and I will go alone, then come back for you when I have found help."

"No!" she shouted, "do not leave me."

Delia clung to the lapels of his coat, not altogether certain he would not turn and leave on the instant. Being trapped here with the major was bad enough, but the idea of remaining behind while he went for help was sufficient to send her to the brink of panic. "You have my w . . . word, Major. I will obey you."

"In everything?" he asked.

"In everything," she replied.

Before many minutes passed, Delia would live to regret that promise. At the moment, however, she was blissfully unaware of what the major would require of her. All she knew was that he was an experienced soldier; moreover, she had every faith in his ability to lead and in her own ability to follow instructions.

"Come," he said again.

He slipped his arm around her shoulders, then led her toward the break in the wall where the gate had once been. "We need not fear being shot at," he said, "for as I said, the men have ridden away, presumably to get themselves out of the elements and into more comfortable surroundings."

Delia did not care why the murderers had gone, nor what their destination. It was enough for her peace of mind that they were no longer out there watching, a loaded pistol at the ready.

The major's arm was still around her shoulders, and to her surprise he walked her all the way to the edge of the moat, close enough that she could see where the earth had broken away when the iron spikes had been kicked loose. Not that she wanted to see it! Or to be that close to the edge! She disliked heights even more than she disliked deep water.

Reacting much as she had done when she had witnessed William's murder, Delia did not turn away. Some macabre fascination kept her in place, and though a shiver ran up her spine, she could not stop herself from looking across at what remained of the footbridge.

The remnants of the planks and rope hung against the far side of the moat, resembling nothing so much as an eerie, ghostlike ladder. The end that had once been secured near where she stood, dangled in the water below, bobbing back and forth as the heavy rains cascaded down the sides of the moat, adding to the menacing depth of the water.

It was while looking at all that swirling, roiling water that Delia got her first suspicion about the major's plan, and why he held her close to his side, his arm still firmly around her shoulder. A sudden surge of nausea made her stomach pitch dangerously. "No!" she said, attempting to push his arm away. "If you are thinking what I suspect you are thinking, I tell you now, I cannot do it. I simply cannot."

The major ignored her protests. "You gave your word, madam, now honor it."

"But—"

"Do exactly as I tell you, and you will come to no harm. On that, you have *my* word."

While he spoke, he released her so he could remove his coat, and now he tied one sleeve end around her left wrist, knotting it very tightly.

She tried to pull away. "What are you doing?"

He did not answer, merely continued to secure the

knot, while he asked a question of his own. "How are your mathematic skills?"

Mathematics? Confused, Delia shook her head, wondering which of them had gone insane, him or her.

"Listen carefully," he said. "The mote is roughly fifteen feet deep. Your height is what? Five feet, five inches?"

"Seven inches," she corrected.

"Even better," he said, for all the world as if any of this made sense. "My coat, from sleeve end to sleeve end, will add another four feet, and with your arm raised, that is an additional foot. By my estimation, that totals somewhat better than ten and a half feet."

"Ten and a half feet," she repeated, still wondering where all this was leading.

"The water is about eight feet deep," he added quietly, "which means that when I lower you down the side of the moat, you will already be in the water up to your waist before I need to release you. That way, the impact will be lessened, and—"

"Release me!" Delia could barely catch her breath.

"Do not fear," he said, "for I will be right behind you. Furthermore, if you take a deep breath just before I let you go, it should be sufficient for your needs until I can pull you back up to the surface."

"Back up to the—" She could not even *say* the word.

Heaven help her! He meant to drop her into the water, knowing full well she would go under. She would drown!

Panic seized her, for already she felt as if there was no air in her lungs. She had to get away from him before it was too late. She could not go into the water. No matter what, she simply could not do it!

Prepared to put as much distance as possible between them, Delia took a step back. "I . . . I am sorry, Major, but—"

"No. It is I who am sorry." He took both her hands in a gentle but firm grip. "Genuinely sorry. Will you forgive me?"

"Of course, sir, for I am persuaded you meant well. It is just that you do not understand how frightened I am of—" She got no further.

The major was still holding her hands, only now his grasp was no longer gentle, and before Delia realized his intention, he had swung her right off her feet, leaving nothing beneath her but air. He was unbelievably strong, and when next she touched something solid, it was the sides of the moat. To her horror, she dangled there much as the footbridge dangled from the other side.

"Major!" she yelled. "This is insane. I order you to pull me back up!"

Chapter Seven

"*D*o you hear me, sir? Pull me up immediately!"

His answer was to let go of her right hand.

Delia screamed, but before the sound even passed her lips, the major had let go of her left hand as well, the only link between them now the coat whose sleeve was tied around her left wrist. Her brain refused to credit what was happening. One instant she was standing on firm ground, and the next she was swinging above ten feet of roiling water, her entire life dependent upon the strength of a gentleman's coat!

"Please, Major, I am begging you. Do not do this."

Ignoring her pleas, he dropped to his knees, inched his hands up the coat, then slowly lowered her into the water. She screamed again, she could not help it, for this was her worst nightmare come to life.

Just as he had estimated, by the time the coat was fully extended, the water came up to Delia's waist. What he had not bothered to mention was how unbelievably cold the water was; so cold it stole her breath away.

"For the love of heaven," she begged, feeling as though she were trying to reason with one who was insane, "do not let me go."

"Breathe!" the major yelled. "Now!"

Too frightened not to obey, Delia pinched her nose between her thumb and forefinger, then drew in a deep breath through her mouth. An instant later, the major let go of the coat, and she felt herself slip beneath the water. The last thing she saw was Major Holcomb scrambling to his feet and leaping over the side of the moat.

She might as well have had weights tied to her ankles, for she sank like the proverbial stone. She knew she had reached bottom, for one of her half boots had slipped off her foot, and her bare toes scraped painfully against the rubble on the floor of the moat. Following her instincts, she bent her knees and pushed with all the strength in her legs. As if in answer to a prayer, she shot upward.

Her breath gave out before she reached the surface, and by the time her head broke free of the rough water, her lungs were on fire. She managed to drag in only one quick breath before her sodden skirt, abetted by that blasted coat, began pulling her down again. This time she would drown for sure—there could be no question of it. She was as close to panic as made no difference when she felt a strong arm encircle her waist from behind and pull her up again into the air.

"I have you," the major said. "Just relax and let me do all the work."

Relax!

The instruction was so ludicrous Delia nearly laughed. Or she would have done so, if laughter had not been beyond the ability of one who had just swallowed half the filthy water in West Sussex. She was still coughing and sputtering, with water coming from her mouth, her nose, her eyes, and perhaps her ears as well, when she felt herself being pushed rather roughly against the far side of the moat.

"Grab hold!" the major yelled.

At first, Delia did not understand the order, then she realized the round thing poking a hole in her face was a rope knot. The footbridge! How they had made it to the dangling bridge she did not know, but she had never been so glad to see anything in her life. As though greeting a long-lost sister, she grabbed the closest plank and wrapped her arms around the battered wood in a hug of desperation. If she had her way, she and that plank would grow old together, still with her arms wrapped around it.

Mitchell knew how terrified she was, so he let her hold to the plank for a short while before he told her to let go. "You need to climb now," he said. "I will remain in the water until you are free, just in case the bridge will no longer support the weight of the two of us."

She either did not or could not understand the request. Not that he blamed her. After what he had done to her, she had a right to be distrustful. Even so, they had to get out of this cold water or soon their fingers would be too stiff to grasp the ropes.

"You must climb," he said directly into her ear. "It is the only way out."

"I . . . I cannot!"

"There is no time for argument. Let go of the plank, Dee, and climb."

"No," she said, desperation in her voice. "I will not let go, and you cannot make me."

He *could* make her, of course, but it would be best not to further deplete her strength or his own. "You have one last chance," he said, hating himself for what he meant to say next. "I will count to five. After that, if you have not moved, I promise you I will climb over you and leave you down here to drown."

That last threat did the trick, for she released one arm and reached up for the next board.

"Hold to the ropes," he yelled, "the boards will have splinters."

When she did as he told her, Mitchell caught his breath, slipped below the water again, and came up quickly, his shoulder beneath her *derriere*. The boost set her a good three feet higher on the "ladder," and though she had to battle fatigue, cold, and a long skirt that did everything possible to get in her way, in a short time she had reached the rim of the moat.

"Grab hold of the iron spikes," he yelled, "and pull yourself over the top. Do not be afraid. If you should fall, I am here to catch you."

"Fi . . . fine words," she said, her teeth chattering so badly he could barely understand her, "from the man who threw me in."

The instant her feet disappear over the top, Mitchell caught hold of the ropes and began his own climb. He made it with little difficulty, but once he reached the top, he was so grateful to be out of the frigid water that it was all he could do not to drop to his knees and kiss the earth.

For fully five minutes after their escape, they lay on the rain-soaked ground, filling their lungs and allowing the rapid beating of their hearts to slow to something like a normal pace. The rain had slackened, and when it stopped entirely, Mitchell finally got to his feet and reached down for Dee.

"I know you are exhausted," he said, "and by right you should be allowed all the time you need to rest. Unfortunately, we cannot remain here, for Georgie and his pal could return at any moment."

To his surprise, she did not protest, but allowed him to catch her by her upper arms and help her to her feet. He held her steady, thinking to give her legs a chance to get accustomed to sustaining her weight, but she surprised him again by pulling her arms from his grasp and stepping out of his reach.

"Leave me alone," she said softly, then she turned her back to him.

Mitchell knew an apology was in order, but for the life of him, he could not think how to begin. How did one apologize for tossing a person into her worst nightmare?

"Dee, I . . ."

He paused, hoping the proper words would come to him, but to his regret, his mind was a complete blank. Finally, wanting only to get it over with, he cleared his throat and tried again. "Dee, you cannot possibly know how sorry I am for what I did. If I could have thought of some other way to get us away from that deuced fort, believe me, I would have done it. I can only imagine what an ordeal that must have been for you, and I hope you can find it in your heart to forgive—"

He got no further, for she whirled suddenly, her eyes alight with anger, and the fingers of her right hand bunched into a fist. Before he could prepare himself for what was to come, she hit him with considerable force, square on his chin. The unexpectedness of the blow rocked his head back and very nearly knocked him off his feet.

"Damnation!" he said, once the spots quit dancing before his eyes.

"I forgive you," she said at last. "But never do that again!"

Chapter Eight

"I agree," Delia said. "Sky Cottage is out of the question. In all likelihood, those two villains are there now."

"Even if they rode all the way to the village, once they determine that we are no longer hiding in the hill fort, the cottage is the first place they will look for us."

"My thoughts exactly. So?" she said, "where do you suggest we go?"

"Me? I had hoped *you* would suggest some place the thugs would not know to look. Surely you have friends in the neighborhood, someone willing to take us in until we can contact the proper authorities."

She shook her head. "I have no friends here."

"But Ems Regis is your home. There must be someone who would—"

"There is no one."

The words held a decided finality, and though Mitchell thought it strange that a young woman who had been reared in Ems Regis, and whose grandmother lived there still, could not call on a single villager for help in an emergency, he was obliged to accept her word on the matter. As for going into the village itself, that was out of the question. "Perhaps we should go to Chichester."

"How far is that?" she asked. "Do you know?"

He knew, of course, he was just surprised that she did not. "Since we traveled north from the cottage for perhaps three miles, I would guess Chichester to be no more than six or seven miles from our present location."

"Oh," she said, disappointment in her voice. "That far."

"Not much of a walker, eh?"

She answered by looking down at her feet, and for the first time Mitchell noticed that one of her half boots was missing. One need not be a genius to guess how and when she had lost the item, and he, being a firm believer in letting sleeping dogs lie, did not remark upon the shoe's absence. Instead, he attempted to add a positive note. "Once we arrive at Chichester, I can hire a conveyance of some kind to take us to Fernbourne, which is quite near."

Fernbourne House. After what Mitchell had been through in the past twenty-four hours, he positively longed for his home, where dry clothes, a warm bed, and hot food awaited him. As if on cue, his stomach roared like a wild beast. And no wonder. He had been drugged before supper, cudgeled before breakfast, marooned in an ancient hill fort before nuncheon, then socked in the chin before tea.

He was tired, he ached in more places than he cared to think about, he was wet and cold, and two men he had never seen before that day wanted to kill him. By his reckoning, if a man ever deserved a decent tea, that man was Mitchell Holcomb!

Fully aware that the closest food and shelter were at least six miles away, he loosened the sleeve that was still knotted around Dee Eskew's wrist, then held the coat out so she could put it on. "It would be of no use for me to offer you my boots, for they would never stay on your small feet. But allow me to offer you my coat."

She stared at him as though he had lost his mind.

"I daresay you mean to be gallant, but the gesture would mean more if the proffered garment were not dripping wet. In its present state, it cannot provide me with even a modicum of warmth."

"Please," he said, offering the coat a second time, "just slip your arms in, there's a good girl."

"I told you I do not want it. And just so we understand one another, Major, any foolish promises I made about obeying you are no longer in effect. Not now. Not ever."

"Even so, madam, I cannot think that you would wish to be seen in your present state. Your bodice . . ." He said no more, for she had looked down at the thin fabric that now clung to her shapely breasts, leaving little to the imagination.

After a quickly swallowed gasp, she turned her back to him. Then, without further protest, she slipped her arms through the sleeves, pulled the coat close, and worked the polished-brass buttons through the buttonholes.

Since there was nothing more Mitchell could do for her, he turned and began walking northward. He did not even look back to see if she followed him, but before he had gone more than a few yards he heard her uneven footfalls on the wet ground. She said not a word, and for the next hour the only sound was her rhythmic *step, squish. Step, squish. Step, squish.*

It was understandable that a woman with one shoe and one bare foot could not walk as fast or as far as a man in possession of a pair of good boots—even a man who had recently used his leg to kick away two iron spikes. Still, Mitchell was surprised that Dee kept pace with him for as long as she did, and all without complaint. He would say this for her, she was no whiner!

For the first half mile, she had even whistled snatches of a tune called "Rambler's Joy." Not that there was much joy in their rambling. Only mud and more mud. No matter, she was making the effort, which was more than he could say for many a raw recruit he had commanded.

They walked fully two miles, up one side of a hill and down the other side, repeating the process again and again across the seemingly never-ending downs. All they saw were scattered groups of the small, white-faced South Down sheep, placidly grazing the hillsides; still, Dee never once questioned his ability to lead them to civilization.

At one point they came upon a particularly boggy meadow where yellow-green coltsfoot grew in abundance, and lemony primrose had begun to peek out from the hedgerows. If nothing else, crossing that boggy stretch made them long for a return of the hills.

Luckily, once they left the boggy meadow, they discovered an old carter's route, heavily rutted and overgrown with gorse, yet still clear enough to follow. They remained on that unused route for at least a mile, until it led them to a country lane that appeared fairly well traveled.

They had only just begun to traverse the country lane when Mitchell heard the dull *clop, clop* of slowly plodding hooves and the unmistakable rattle of wagon wheels. "With any luck," he said, turning to look behind them, "we may get a ride the remainder of the way."

The sigh of relief that escaped Dee's lips told its own story, and because Mitchell knew all too well the trials she had endured that day, he put his arm around her shoulders and gave them a reassuring squeeze. Immediately, she pushed him away.

"Oh, no," she said. "Keep your distance, sir, for I am not the fool you think me."

Understandably confused, he asked her what she meant.

"The last time you put your arm around my shoulder, I nearly drowned. If it is your plan to stop that wagon by tossing me in front of the horses, I tell you now I will not be sacrificed a second time."

With the best resolve in the world, Mitchell could not keep from laughing. "Believe it or not, such an idea never crossed my mind. Though now that you mention it, such a ploy might prove most effect— *Oof*!"

Her elbow connected rather forcefully with his solar plexus, and though he still laughed, he backed away before she decided to try fisticuffs again. As it happened, she offered no further physical threat, and by the time the creaky old farm wagon finally rolled into view, she was visibly sagging against a small holm oak tree, all her energy apparently spent.

There was but one horse, a dun-colored, sway-backed mare, and all Mitchell had to do to induce the weary animal to pause was to touch its neck. The awestruck driver, a farm lad of perhaps seventeen, offered no protest to being stopped; he merely sat on the plank seat, his eyes wide as saucers and his mouth agape. He had obviously hauled swine in the past few hours, for the bowed wagon, which resembled nothing so much as a flat-bottomed boat on wheels, still retained the odor of that pink-snouted creature.

"Good day to you," Mitchell said in what he hoped was a winning manner. "Thank you for stopping."

The youth's mouth fell open even wider, and it crossed Mitchell's mind that the fellow might be addlepated. Not that it mattered. At this point, Mitchell would gladly accept a ride from an escaped bedlamite.

"I hope I find you well . . . er, I am sorry, lad, I am certain we have met before, but I do not recall your name. My memory is not what it used to be."

"Name's Diggs," he replied, finding his tongue at last. "Paulie Diggs. But I don't recall—"

"Ah, yes, Diggs, now I remember." So far so good! "I was wondering, Paulie, if you were headed for Chichester?"

"Ch'ester? No, sir. Ma don't let me take the wagon no place but Ems Regis, and I just come from there. I'm for home, 'fore the rain comes again. Besides, Ma'll be waiting supper."

Mitchell had been too concerned with finding their way to pay close attention to the weather, but now he noticed the clouds were back again, and they looked thicker and blacker than ever. He doubted Dee Eskew could make it another mile under ideal conditions; it was asking too much of her to expect her to trudge through a downpour. She needed to rest in some warm, sheltered place, and like him, she needed food.

Nothing if not resilient, Mitchell changed tactics. If the lad could not take them to Chichester, they would go where he could take them. "Did you say something about supper, Paulie?"

The youth nodded, a big smile revealing several gaps in his front teeth. "Tonight we be having pork pasties with onions and turnips. They be my favorites."

"Mine as well," Mitchell said. Strictly speaking, the remark was not true, but considering the gnawing inside his stomach, anything edible would figure as his favorite meal. "Do you suppose your mother would be willing to feed my . . . er, wife and me? I can pay."

To prove the statement, he reached inside his waistcoat pocket, where he usually carried a few shillings for tips. To his dismay, he found only one coin, and it was not a shilling. "I have sixpence," he said, holding up the small silver coin and hoping the youth would think it a handsome sum. "What say you? Will you take us to your mother?"

While Paulie pondered the unusual request, Mitchell caught Dee's hand and more or less dragged her around to the rear of the wagon. Her energy had flagged considerably in the few minutes since they had stopped walking, and now she had difficulty putting one foot in front of the other.

"Just a little farther," he said, lifting her in his arms and setting her in the filthy wagon bed. It was a testament to her fatigue that she did not even protest his high-handedness. As for the lingering swine aroma, not to mention the suspicious clumps that decorated the hay-strewn floor, she seemed oblivious to both.

"Drive on," Mitchell called, once he had hopped aboard.

The youngster turned then, indecision on his homely face. "I b'aint so sure Ma'll like me bringing strangers to—"

"Paulie, my boy," Mitchell said in what was meant to be a reassuring voice, "I promise you, your mother will be delighted."

Paulie may have been a little indecisive about extending hospitality to the weary travelers, but his mother was made of sterner stuff, and she was quick to take the measure of such a bedraggled-looking pair. She was probably no more than thirty-five, but hard work and poverty had etched lines of suspicion around what had once been a pretty mouth.

"Paulie Diggs!" she cried when the boy halted the tired mare before a small cottage whose roof badly needed rethatching and whose oak entrance door hung drunkenly on its hinges. "Have you taken leave of your senses? That there's a Gypsy in our wagon. You want we should be murdered in our beds?"

Mitchell, hoping to allay the woman's fears, jumped to the ground and made her his most courtly bow. "How do you do, Mrs. Diggs? Pray, allow me to introduce myself. I am Major Mitchell Holcomb, late of His Majesty's service.

The woman eyed him with all the trust of an ill-treated hound. "Save your playacting for babes and fools. If you're a major, then I'm one of them French *modistes*." She laughed at her own humor, though the laughter never quite reached her eyes. "You're trying to gull me, but it won't work. I b'aint one as takes a goose for a swan, and I know a major wouldn't be traveling around on foot, unshaven and dirty. And where's your hat and coat, soldier boy? I won't even ask how come that Gypsy gal you got with you has only one shoe."

Obviously, the mother had the brains in the family, and unless Mitchell could appeal to her better nature—assuming she had one—he and Dee would be walking again very soon.

"You are very observant, Mrs. Diggs. As I was telling young Paulie, my wife and I—"

The woman *humphed* when he had said "wife," obviously not fooled in the least, but he continued with his story. "We met with a mishap on the road. A pair of villains robbed us, and we have been traveling most of the day, trying to reach Chichester. We stand before you wet and hungry, but we are far from beggars."

He removed the sixpence from his waistcoat pocket and held it toward her. "I understand you have made pasties for dinner, and I should be happy to pay you for a share."

She eyed the coin with apparent pleasure. "One pastie," she said, snatching the coin from his fingers, "but you'll have to eat it outside. I don't let strangers in my house."

"You are wise, ma'am, to be so cautious. But—"

"No 'buts' about it. You b'aint coming inside, and that's an end to it. I got a blunderbuss, and I b'aint afraid to use it."

A large, cold raindrop splattered on Mitchell's hand, and when it was followed by a clap of thunder that literally shook the earth beneath his feet, he made up his mind that unless the inhospitable woman made good her threat and held him at gunpoint, he was not budging from the premises until the next day. "As I was about to tell you, ma'am, my wife and I will be quite happy to share the horse's accommodations. You do have a barn, I presume?"

"Yes, sir," Paulie informed him. "We got a barn. Only it's got a—"

"You shut your mummer!" his devoted parent instructed him, "and let me think."

Slowly, her eyes took on an avaricious glow. "You and your *missus* can stay in the barn for tonight. But it'll cost you extra. And that Gypsy gal b'aint to come nowhere near the cottage, else I'll fetch the blunderbuss."

Dee climbed down from the wagon, and as she stood beside it, her head held high, Mrs. Diggs's attention was caught by the two rows of polished-brass buttons on the coat.

"Them's nice buttons," she said.

As if needing no time to consider the matter, Dee yanked off the entire left row of buttons—one, two, three, four—then held them palm up toward the woman. "They are yours," she said with a quiet dignity that Mitchell could not help but admire. "The first two are for allowing us to stay in your barn until morning. The other two are for lending us blankets."

The woman snatched the buttons from Dee's hand, almost as if afraid to touch her. "Two blankets," she said, apparently eager to seal the bargain, "and you leave at first light."

As it turned out, the barn left much to be desired. The old mare occupied one of the two stalls, and unless Mitchell's nose was playing him false, the second stall had once been the bailiwick of the recently relocated swine. As if the odor was not enough of a obstacle to human comfort, a section of the back wall had rotted through, leaving a gaping hole through which

rain and wind traveled unimpaired. The hole was possibly the imperfection Paulie had tried to confess, and
Mitchell was not at all surprised that Mrs. Diggs had
told the lad to be quiet.

"At least," Dee said, "it is shelter."

Though appreciative of her forbearance, Mitchell
made a concerted effort to plug the hole. After bringing in a rain barrel so full of cracks and fissures it was
incapable of holding water, he fitted the barrel into
the hole, then chinked around it with a few dozen
handfuls of straw. When the job was finished, Dee
told him the place would do nicely.

They had divided evenly the single pork pastry and
a mug of home brew, and once every last crumb was
consumed and every drop of the thick, bitter brew
drunk, Mitchell told Dee to take off her clothes.

"What!"

Exhaustion sat heavily upon her, and she had been
struggling for the past half hour to keep her eyelids
open. At his order to disrobe, however, she came fully
awake, the determined set of her chin indicating her
willingness to fight tooth and claw to preserve her
virtue.

"You may relax," Mitchell said, "for I have no de-
signs upon you. After the day we had, Salome could
eschew her seven veils and dance naked in front of
me, and I would not bat so much as an eyelid. Believe
me, madam, you are quite safe."

Delia did not know whether to be relieved or insulted. In her wildest dreams, she had never pictured
herself dancing naked in front of a man. Now that she
gave it some thought, however, the least she would
expect from the unnamed audience of one was that
he show a little interest in the performance.

While she hesitated, the major threw her one of the
blankets his brass buttons had leased for the night.

"What I meant to suggest, Dee, had I not been too
tired to think straight, was that while I muck out the

empty stall and refurbish it with fresh hay, you might want to take off your wet things, wrap yourself in the blanket, then hang your clothes somewhere so they can dry by morning."

It was a sensible suggestion, and Delia felt a fool for having thought he meant anything else. "An excellent idea."

With that settled, it finally penetrated her own tired brain that there was only the one stall, and that the major obviously expected them to share the space. Speechless with embarrassment at the very thought of so offending the proprieties, she looked all around her, hoping to find some empty spot where she could curl up alone. To her chagrin, in such a tiny barn no such spot existed. She must either share the stall or sit upright in the corner near the rain barrel.

As it turned out, once the stall was clean and ready for use, all she could think about was lying down and closing her eyes. With the blanket wrapped securely around her, she was warm for the first time in hours, and after she had banished from her mind all thoughts of observing proper decorum, she stretched out on the hay, where she fell asleep mid-yawn. She was aware of nothing and no one until a cock crowed at first light the next day.

At first, Delia had no idea where she was. All she knew with any certainty was that she felt rested and deliciously warm. Of course, any woman would feel warm with a muscular arm wrapped around her waist and a man's hard, unyielding body molded to hers in a way that made them fit together like a pair of spoons in a drawer. She had never been this close to a man before; even so, she knew without doubt that the average man did not possess as fine a physique as the one burning its imprint into her body.

His chest was broad and sheltering against her back—a circumstance that infused her with a delicious indolence—while the legs that nestled snugly behind her legs were long and undeniably powerful, sending an unexpected heat throughout her entire body. His mouth was very close to her earlobe, and his rhythmic breathing caused a tingling sensation all along the side of her neck—a tingling so pleasant she wished it would go on forever.

Still half asleep, Delia turned her head so the warm breath caressed her cheek. "Umm," she murmured, pleased with this new area of sensation.

She did not want to risk breaking contact with the enveloping masculine warmth, but it crossed her sleep-fogged brain that by lifting her chin the least little bit, she could get her mouth closer to the mouth that was even now tempting her to come explore. Inviting her to come take her fill.

More than willing to accept the invitation, she had just begun to lift her chin when the arm that fit so perfectly around her waist was suddenly snatched away. Before she knew what was happening, the hand came up to grasp her shoulder firmly, almost painfully, blocking her from turning further. "Be still," he said.

His voice was hoarse from sleep, but none the less adamant. "It is early yet," he added. "Go back to sleep."

At the sound of his voice, Delia realized who held her so intimately, and she froze, not moving, not even daring to breathe. She had thought she was dreaming. Unfortunately, it was no dream, and the masculine body wrapped around hers was all too real. With painful clarity, memories of everything that had happened the day before came rushing back to her, and all vestiges of sleep disappeared.

She was in a dilapidated old barn. She was naked except for a single blanket. And she was snuggled body to body with Mitchell Holcomb!

Sleep had freed her from her inhibitions, and she had come as close as makes no difference to throwing herself at Mitchell Holcomb's head. Mortified at the recollection of her wantonness, Delia hid her face in the crook of her arm, attempted a soft snoring sound, and pretended she was still asleep.

Moments later, he drew away from her, then got up altogether. Delia heard him moving about the barn, gathering up his clothes, then working his feet into his boots. Still feigning sleep, she waited until he opened the barn door and went outside before she turned onto her back and stared at the still-gray dawn inching its way around the plugged hole in the wall.

Her entire body burned with embarrassment. What must he think of her? Most likely he was repulsed by her wanton behavior. Otherwise, why had he been in such a rush to get away from her?

Chapter Nine

*T*hey sat just outside the Diggs's barn, neither of
them speaking. As the silence stretched between
them, they watched the sky make the transition from
dawn gray to morning blue. Dee Eskew was perched
on a tree stump, while Mitchell made do with an overturned bucket. He had bartered with Mrs. Diggs for
another meal of sorts—two slices of coarse brown
bread spread with butter—and after eating his portion,
he had brought the other slice to Dee.

She had taken the bread and butter and thanked
him, but she had avoided looking him in the eyes.
And he knew why. She was embarrassed at what had
almost happened earlier.

Without knowing it, she had slept for most of the
night with her soft, pliant body flush against his,
a circumstance that had awakened him more than
once. Each time he had been obliged to turn away
from her before he disgraced himself by acting
upon the impulses kindled by their closeness. That
last time had been different, however, for she had
awakened first—or half awakened—while he had
slept on.

Mitchell had been enjoying a most delightful dream,
one in which a soft, deliciously rounded female was
in his arms, snuggled so close they were very nearly

one flesh. When the real-life female moved slightly against him, he came awake with a start.

Instantly he wanted her. Even before he realized it was Dee Eskew he held, he wanted her. Even after he remembered that it was Dee, he wanted her. He reminded himself that she was a woman under his protection, and that no gentleman worthy of the name would dream of taking advantage of the situation, and still he wanted her.

He had remained perfectly still, hoping she would drift off again so he could move away from her without her realizing he had been there. Unfortunately, it had not worked out that way. Every inch of his body was already aware of every inch of hers, and when she turned her head, lifting her chin the least little bit, almost as if seeking his kiss, he knew he had to get away from her with all due haste.

Everything in him cried out to take the kiss, and anything else she offered, and it was all he could do to reach up, take her shoulder, and stop her from turning to him. She was exhausted both physically and mentally, and in that vulnerable state the last thing she needed was to make a decision based on her need for comfort.

Mitchell had breathed a sigh of relief when she put her face in her arm and pretended to be asleep. Seizing the opportunity, he had broken the contact and scurried away—thankfully, before he forgot that he was supposedly a man of honor.

Now she could not look at him, and Mitchell had to do something to divert her thoughts from what almost happened between them.

"You will be pleased to know," he began, "that Mrs. Diggs has agreed to let her son take us in the farm wagon all the way to Fernbourne House, which is just beyond Chichester."

Surprised, Delia looked up from her meager meal. "How did you manage that?"

"I gave her my coat, which she means to sell, and I promised to give Paulie my boots once we reach our destination."

"That was good of you," she said. And she meant it, for it was quite generous of him.

She had no idea what sort of funds a retired army officer had at his disposal, but with the present financial status of the government, she was certain his pension could not be much, even if he had been fortunate enough to receive prize money. As well, she knew little of the price of gentlemen's clothing, but unless she missed her guess, he had not gotten those boots for less than fifty pounds.

The major had sacrificed both his coat and his boots, and since she was the one having the most difficulty covering the miles, Delia knew he had made the bargain more for her benefit than his own. He was bearing the expense of their escape, without even knowing why they needed to escape, and she felt guilty about both the expense and the continued subterfuge.

Silently she vowed to repay him every last pence just as soon as she had access to her bank. Of course, she had no idea when that would be. For now she had no money, and the question that weighed heaviest on her mind was where she would go once they reached Chichester. London was out of the question, and for the time being at least, Nadja's cottage was equally unsafe.

Not wanting to think about what was to become of her once they reached the end of their journey, Delia concentrated on the major, who was coatless and soon to be bootless. Though she tried to push it aside, a rather amusing image began to form in her mind— a picture of the formerly well-dressed major strolling barefoot down the streets of the little village he called home.

When she could no longer hide her smile, he asked her what she found so amusing.

"I was wondering, sir, what your neighbors will say when they see you sans coat and shoes."

He chuckled. "I can see the idea of my embarrassment has you nearly in tears. You are not to worry, however, for I am unlikely to be seen by any neighbors."

No neighbors? The comment struck Delia as odd, for she had assumed that this Fernbourne House he spoke of with such affection in his voice must be an establishment that specialized in leasing rooms to bachelors. Perhaps exclusively to retired military officers.

She was to remember this quite erroneous assumption later, when she and Mitchell Holcomb were once again passengers in the back of the Diggs farm wagon. As before, Paulie sat on the hard plank seat, the reins in hand, while the ancient mare pulled the wagon as placidly as though she had traveled that same route a million times.

Unlike the horse, the lad was far from placid. Excitement at traveling to a new place was evident in the way his head turned slowly from side to side, his mouth a perfect O in amazement. As they approached the large and prosperous market town of Chichester, he seemed to gobble up each new sight, each new view of the shops and coaching inns, like one starved for a change of routine. Like a visitor to some strange new world, the boy stared in wonder at the many cobbled streets and alleys and the hundreds of people abroad.

Following the major's instructions, Paulie did not drive past the beautiful old Norman cathedral. Instead, he turned onto a narrow, twisting street that led them past Chichester's sixteenth-century market cross, one of the finest in England. The cross had been built to invoke God's blessing upon the trade of the town, and when the wagon rattled on, leaving Chichester behind and continuing not toward another village

but toward a private estate, Delia silently asked for a
bit of that blessing for herself.

Where, exactly, was the major taking her? Surely
his lodgings were close to the town.

"Just around the next bend, Paulie, you will want
to turn to the right."

The lad looked down at his hands, as if trying to
determine which was his right. Seeing the lad's dilemma, the major smiled. "Not to worry, lad. You will
see the gates shortly."

And see them they did. How could they not? Not
when the gates were constructed of beautifully
wrought Italian iron. It was a magnificent entrance,
and beyond it the curving, crushed-stone carriageway
bisected a sweeping greensward. To the right, the rolling lawn ended at a formal, walled garden, while to
the left it gave access to a pretty wilderness area that
was enhanced by the addition of several rustic
wooden benches.

Even with the grounds bearing testimony to the
splendor and prosperity of the estate, Delia was not
prepared for the grandeur of the house. The edifice
was four-storied, possessed wings to both the east and
the west, and she judged the whole to contain upwards
of fifty rooms.

A pleasingly symmetrical mansion, it had been built
around the mid-seventeenth century. The building had
been lovingly preserved, somehow escaping the usual
hideous additions thought necessary by subsequent
generations of owners. Though whether that was a
result of good judgment, or just plain luck, Delia
dared not ask.

The brick, mellowed to a silvery pink hue, was laid
in a herringbone pattern, and above the oak entrance,
which had blackened with age, the letter *F* had been
cleverly worked into the design. Delia stared in
amazement at the house, much as Paulie had done
when viewing Chichester.

Who, she wondered, was the family represented by that initial above the door? Surely this was not Fernbourne House! The moment the thought entered her head, Delia knew it was true. Fernbourne was not a lodging house but a private residence.

Was the major visiting some friend here? Or perhaps some wealthy, distant relative outside the Holcomb family? One thing was certain, no matter what the major's connection to the owner, this beautifully maintained property belonged to a person of considerable substance.

"Stop at the entrance, Paulie."

"Aye, sir."

When they stopped, the major removed first one boot then the other and tossed them behind him on the wagon. "I am leaving the boots as I promised, Paulie. Wear them in good health."

"Thankee, sir."

"Thank *you*," he replied. "You are quite certain you can find your way home?"

"Aye, sir. Once I've been to a place, I do just fine."

"Good lad."

After jumping down, then helping Delia to alight, he told Paulie to follow the carriageway around to the kitchen. "Tell Cook I sent you, and she will give you some refreshment before you drive home."

The wagon had already begun to move again when Delia finally found her voice. "Perhaps we should go around to the kitchen as well."

"Whatever for?"

"If for no other reason, because I can just imagine the butler's shocked expression if I should present myself at the main entrance."

The major seemed surprised. "What foolishness is this? Butlers are paid to admit guests, not pass judgment on them."

Men! Did they live in another world?

"For the love of heaven, Mitchell, look at me. Even

if I were clean—which I am not—I would not be appropriately dressed for entering such an establishment as this. I am filthy, and what is worse, I smell of the stables."

"True. But, then, so do I."

She sighed, exasperated with him for acting so obtuse. "It is not the same, and you know it, for you are acquainted with these people. I am a complete stranger."

"You are acquainted with me," he said. "That is sufficient."

"It is far from sufficient. Have you forgotten how Mrs. Diggs reacted to the sight of me?"

He muttered an oath beneath his breath. "Forget about the Diggs woman. She was a bucolic opportunist, whose small cottage was a perfect match to the smallness of her mind."

"Be that as it may, the owner of this grand house might well share her opinion."

"He will not."

"You cannot know that."

"I can," he said, "for I am the owner."

Chapter Ten

*I*f her life had depended upon it, Delia could not have said how she got from the wagon to the green-and-white-marbled vestibule of Fernbourne House. She remembered the major's revelation, that he owned this palatial estate, and she recalled feeling as if she had been turned to stone. Other than that, everything was a blur until she stood beneath the cut-crystal chandelier in the spacious vestibule, a very superior-looking butler staring down his nose at her.

"Good afternoon, Newly."

The tall, middle-aged servant inclined his head in what passed for a bow. "Good afternoon, sir. I hope I find you well."

"Quite well, thank you."

The servant's expression remained impassive, as if it was nothing out of the ordinary for his master to disappear for the better part of two days, then return unshaven, unwashed, and unshod. "The post is in your book room, sir, along with some periodicals brought by Lady Regina."

"Brought?"

"Yes, sir. Her ladyship arrived yesterday morning, not long after you left. She is in the blue withdrawing room at the moment, enjoying a dish of tea. Shall I inform her that you are returned?"

Lady Regina! Delia hoped she had misheard.

"You may inform her later, Newly. I cannot think my mother would wish to see me until I am much more presentable."

His mother? Delia stifled a groan. It wanted only that!

"For now," the major continued, "please see that hip baths and a great deal of hot water are prepared. One tub for the master suite and the other for Miss Eskew. Is the yellow bedchamber available?"

"It is, sir, for her ladyship's guests do not mean to stay overnight."

"Guests? Damnation! Never tell me my mother is entertaining."

"Not until dinner, sir. Lady Yarborough's cousin is at The Park for a fortnight's stay, and Lady Regina has arranged a card party in the gentleman's honor. It is a small gathering, with no more than a dozen expected to sit down to dinner. I am persuaded her ladyship will be pleased to know that you have returned, for she was hoping you would act as host for the evening."

The major muttered something unintelligible, then sighed as if already resigned to the inevitable. "You may inform my mother that I will be happy to host the dinner, but that I refuse to play cards. Besides, I have brought a guest."

He motioned toward Delia, who felt her cheeks flame. "Please," she said, "do not forgo the evening's entertainment on my account."

"Believe me, Dee, one does not speak of entertainment and my mother's card parties in the same breath. Especially when Lady Yarborough, who is one of her particular friends, is to be among the numbers. A truly incompetent player, my neighbor insists upon playing silver loo for chicken stakes, and upon one occasion it is said she sulked for weeks because she lost ten pounds in one evening."

He returned his attention to the butler. "As you

have no doubt concluded, Newly, Miss Eskew will require a maid to wait upon her for the duration of her visit. I leave the selection of the servant to you. As well, I trust Mrs. Newly can find clothes and the like to make our guest comfortable?"

Not by so much as a flared nostril did the butler betray his misgivings about showing a bedraggled Gypsy to one of the principal guest chambers, nor about having his wife attend to her needs. "It shall be as you ask, sir."

"Oh, and have a couple of trays sent up as well. With some sandwiches and cakes, and—what say you, Miss Eskew?—a pot of tea?"

Delia would have liked to refuse, but considering the meager amount of food she had consumed in the past twenty-four hours, she could not keep the sound of anticipation from her voice. "Tea would be lovely."

The yellow bedchamber was a large, beautifully appointed apartment, with Chinese silk paper on the walls, satin hangings at the bed and windows, and a deep-piled Axminster carpet on the floor. Such elegance was guaranteed to welcome the most exacting visitor, but what interested Delia most was the hip bath that had been set before the fireplace. The thought of being warm and clean was absolute heaven.

She scrubbed herself from her scalp to her toes, and after a quarter of an hour's soak, she was ready to swear that soap and hot water would cure most of the world's ills. Not that her renewed cleanliness had effected the understandably cool treatment she received from the housekeeper, Mrs. Newly. Nor, in all likelihood, would it guarantee any warmer reception when she finally met Lady Regina Holcomb.

Of course, she had no one but herself to blame for the situation. After all, she had presented herself to the major as the granddaughter of Nadja Eskew. Having claimed to be a Gypsy, she could not complain when she was treated as one, and not like a lady; especially by servants accustomed to waiting upon members of the peerage.

After the revelation that this beautiful estate belonged to Major Holcomb, and that his mother was the daughter of the Earl of Brentford, a wealthy and highly respected peer, Delia was obliged to revise her original assumption that the major viewed William's son, Robbie, as an inconvenient heir. Obviously, Mitchell was *not* counting the days until he became heir to his uncle's less significant estate and title.

According to Betty, the gossipy maid who had helped her with the bath, Mitchell had long been a most sought-after gentleman, a real matrimonial prize. Not only because of his good looks and affable manners, but also because he was the sole heir of Lord Fernbourne, who was both his godfather and his second cousin on his mother's side. Three years ago, while still serving in the Peninsula, Mitchell had inherited Fernbourne House, plus a smaller estate in Shropshire, and a fortune that even the most reserved of the *ton* would call handsome.

An earl's grandson, even one without a title of his own, was viewed by the world as a *premier parti*. Add to his distinguished lineage two prosperous estates and money of his own, and it was highly unlikely that Mitchell was pining away for Sir Allistair's estate, nor desirous of the baronet's title.

Now that she had the facts, Delia was embarrassed to recall that she had suspected Mitchell of wanting to do away with William's infant son so that *he* could remain his uncle's heir. Mitchell was wealthy in his own right—presumably far wealthier than his uncle, Sir Allistair—and chances were he had come to Ems Regis out of family loyalty. Not to harm Robbie, but to prove or disprove the child's legitimacy before presenting him to his grandfather.

Witnessing William's murder had made Delia suspicious of everyone. Even so, the past twenty-four hours spent in Mitchell Holcomb's company should have convinced her that he was a man of honor. He had been drugged because she suspected him, attacked because he defended her, and shot at for helping her escape.

And yet, when she needed him he had not turned his back on her. He had protected her from the two thugs who wished to murder her—at some risk to himself—and after helping her to escape, he had brought her to his home and treated her as an honored guest, all the while believing her to be a Gypsy.

If anyone was without honor, it was Delia.

She had lied to Mitchell about who she was, then she had hidden Robbie from him and denied any knowledge of Cordelia Barrington, the woman he had come to Ems Regis to see. How she was to make everything right, she did not know. Mitchell deserved an explanation, and Delia prayed she would find an opportunity to do so before he discovered the truth on his own. If nothing else, when she left on the morrow, she would leave him a letter explaining everything.

"A Gypsy!" Lady Regina said, the gray eyes so like her son's, wide with incredulity. "You went to Ems Regis on business for your Uncle Allistair, and now you tell me you did not find the little boy or the woman who wrote the letter."

"That is correct."

"You did, however, find a young person whose family consists of one old Gypsy grandmother, and whose worldly goods apparently include nothing more than the clothes on her back and one shoe."

Mitchell smiled. "You were ever a downy one, Mother. I should say that is a pretty fair assessment of my two days' adventure."

"Do not attempt to charm me, Mitchell, for I will not be distracted. Downy indeed!"

Her ladyship sat in a wing chair whose pretty, sky-blue brocade was a perfect backdrop for her salt-and-pepper hair and the English rose complexion that was the envy of all her friends. "This is a serious matter, and you know it, for a man in your position cannot go traipsing about the country with a female in tow. Even a female of low birth."

His mother *tsk-tsked*. "Trust me, dear boy, there will be consequences. Before the cat can lick her ear, someone will show up at your door—it will be a male claiming to be the girl's father or her brother, or even her husband—and he will demand satisfaction for your having compromised this Gypsy person."

"Such an occurrence is highly unlikely, ma'am."

"I hope it may be so. I suspect, however, that when this week is over, you will be poorer by at least a thousand pounds."

He shook his head. "You do not know Dee."

"Nor, I daresay, do you. Men are always such fools when confronted by a pretty face. I daresay she is pretty?"

When he would have answered, she raised her hand as if to silence him. "It does not matter. And since I know you will pay no heed to my warnings, I will say nothing more on the subject."

"I am delighted to hear it, ma'am, for I was beginning to think you had come to Fernbourne only to ring a peal over me."

"Disrespectful boy! I never ring peals."

Mitchell chuckled. "In that case, am I to assume that your visit was occasioned by an attack of maternal affection?"

"You make it sound like a disease. Of course it was motivated by affection. That, and the fact that I was all packed to travel to Tunbridge Wells to meet your father for a fortnight's holiday."

"And my father canceled?"

"It was a matter of great importance to the Crown,

or Parliament, I forget which. He was all apologies, of course, but the trip was postponed none the less. So, I decided to come to Fernbourne instead, to see for myself that you were recuperating satisfactorily from your wound."

"And when you found me absent, you let Lady Yarborough wheedle you into entertaining her cousin with dinner and a card party."

Lady Regina sighed. "Amelia Yarborough and I have been friends for too many years for me to ignore her pleas for support in time of trouble."

"Trouble? Ha! Admit it, Mother, Lady Yarborough is undeniably the laziest hostess in the kingdom, and you are easily the most tenderhearted of women. Are you even acquainted with her cousin?"

His mother shrugged her shoulders, causing the Norwich silk shawl she wore against the late afternoon chill to slip down her arms. "With Lord Leeland? I am acquainted with him, of course, for he is received everywhere. His *ton* is excellent, and as a bachelor he is a hostess's delight, for he is always willing to complete the numbers at table at the last minute. Not to mention being gracious enough to dance with ladies who are short of partners. But to answer your question, his lordship and I are not friends. How could we be when Conrad holds the man in contempt?"

"Since my father is an avid Tory, am I to understand that Lord Leeland is a member of the loyal opposition?"

His mother considered the question. "As to that, I cannot say. I consider him nothing more than an aging coxcomb—he affects a lisp, if you please—though your father has often warned me not to be too hasty in my judgment of the man. If Leeland is political, I have no knowledge of the fact. I am the wife of a member of Parliament, but my interest in politics begins and ends with Conrad Holcomb."

"Nothing to be ashamed of, ma'am."

Lady Regina's eyebrows shot up as though she was shocked. "I said nothing of being ashamed. I merely stated the obvious, that I make no claim to being one of those celebrated political hostesses."

Her son raised her hand to his lips. "And yet, Father and I find you perfect just as you are."

His mother snatched her hand away, but the pleasure in her eyes told its own story. "To return to the subject of Lord Leeland, I believe Conrad mentioned him in one of his letters to me."

"And what did my father have to say?"

"As well as I can remember, the gist of the letter had to do with a group of very powerful men who opposed the Regency Bill, primarily because Prinny is a lifelong Whig. According to your father, those men fear the Regency will result in the fall of the present government."

Mitchell was quiet for a moment, assimilating what his mother had said. "What those powerful men truly fear, I daresay, is a decline in the tremendous profits they are making as a result of the ongoing war with the French. Their continued wealth would depend on the preservation of the status quo."

"Yes, I believe there was some mention of ruinous profiteering. But do not, I pray you, hold me to any particulars."

"There is only one important particular, ma'am. If Prinny should replace the Tory leaders with Whigs, there would be an immediate shake-up, and the war profits would come to an abrupt end. At least for the present profiteers."

Her ladyship adjusted her shawl. "That is as may be, but let us have no more talk of politics. It is your father's guiding passion, not mine. Surely you and I can speak of other things."

Mitchell was not fooled into thinking this directive signaled the introduction of a truly new topic. "What sort of things, ma'am?"

"I wish to know about this Gypsy you have installed in the yellow bedchamber. Why have you brought this person here, to your home, and how long do you mean for her to remain?"

"The first half of your question is easier to answer than the second. I brought Dee Eskew here because she and I were being pursued by a pair of miscreants bent on killing us."

His mother gasped. "Kill you? But why?"

"Their reasons for wishing us dead are as yet a mystery to me. But now that I am home and out of harm's way, and can give the matter the attention it deserves, I mean to discover the answer. More than that I cannot say."

His mother looked at him suspiciously. "Was there really an attempt on your life, or was that just a whisker to give my mind some other direction?"

Mitchell smiled. "A whisker? Why would I wish to redirect your mind?"

"Why? Because of this Dee person. No doubt she is terribly low and vulgar."

"As to that, ma'am, I find her neither. Of course, you may form your own opinion of her later this evening, for I have asked her to join us for dinner and the party afterward."

Lady Regina's mouth fell open. "Attend the party! A Gypsy? Mitchell Holcomb, have you lost your mind? How can you suggest such a—"

"She will need an appropriate frock, of course."

"I should just think she would! From what I was told, the clothes she wore when she arrived were nothing short of a disgra—"

"Then we are agreed," he said, cutting short her diatribe. "May I count on you to be gracious enough to spare her one of your dresses?"

"One of my— Dear boy, what you suggest is preposterous. Not the dress, of course, for I daresay my woman packed at least a dozen. What I beg you to consider is what your neighbors will say if they should discover that a Gypsy had been foisted upon them. Surely a tray in her room would be far more—"

"I have no wish to cross swords with you," Mitchell said, a touch of steel in his voice, "but in my own home, I believe I may please myself as to whom I invite to my table."

His mother had the grace to blush. "You need not bite my head off! Naturally, I should not dream of telling you what to do in your own home, my boy. It is just—"

"She is tall," he said, clearly bringing the discussion to an end, "with a slim, yet womanly figure, and her hair is light brown with gold highlights. As for her eyes, they are a rather striking color, more topaz than brown."

For a moment his mother said nothing. Finally, she exhaled as though she had been holding her breath. "My God! She sounds quite lovely, this Gypsy."

"I will allow you to judge that for yourself, ma'am. That is, if you will lend her something appropriate to wear."

"I will, of course. Only—"

"Something in gold or green, I should think. I trust I may leave the selection to you and your woman?"

Lady Regina nodded, then sighed as if much put upon. "I suppose it is too much to hope that a Gypsy would know which fork to use?"

A wicked grin played on Mitchell's face. "In all honesty, Mother, the only time I saw Dee eat, she made do with her fingers."

With that, Mitchell exited the drawing room, leaving his horrified mother searching in her reticule for her smelling salts.

Chapter Eleven

*T*he dinner dress was bronze colored. It was fashioned of Spitalfields silk, and the long sleeves as well as the hem were banded by crocheted lace of an ocher-brown. Cut and sewn by a master, the creation was deceptively simple, and on first seeing it folded over the arm of Lady Regina's stone-faced dresser, Delia had thought the style far too mature for a lady still on the sunny side of thirty.

Not so the loquacious Betty, who was excited to be called into service as a lady's maid. After assisting Delia to remove the hideous mustard-colored flannel dressing gown Mrs. Newly had deemed appropriate for a female of questionable social standing, the young servant had slipped the dress over Delia's head. Even before the hooks were fastened and the tapes tied, it was apparent the dress was perfect for a woman of Delia's stature and coloring. "Oh, miss," Betty said, "it might have been made for you."

Except for the fact that the square neckline dipped a bit low, revealing more of Delia's bosom than she usually exhibited, the dress fit perfectly. Setting humility aside, she admitted to herself that it was the most becoming dress she had ever worn.

Her freshly washed hair had been brushed until it shone, then arranged in a figure-eight knot at her nape, with loosened tendrils spilling along her temples.

The style was sophisticated, and just the right touch for the dress.

Betty sighed, then stood back to gaze at her in the looking glass. "Mark my words, miss, the gentlemen'll have eyes for none but you."

Delia thanked the maid, but she hoped the prediction did not come true. As an unchaperoned female, presently a guest in the home of an unmarried male, there would be enough of a stir when she was presented to the guests. She could already imagine what her dinner companions would be saying of her behind their fans. She did not wish to invite further tittle-tattle by becoming the center of male attention.

Delia pulled at the low neckline once again. "Deuce take it!" she said, when the material would not be encouraged to cover any more of her exposed flesh. "Is there a fichu?"

The maid appeared horrified by the suggestion of adding so unfashionable a garment. "What you need is a bit of jewelry, miss. Shall I ask Lady Regina's dresser to—"

"No!" She had not meant to yell her reply, but the word slipped out before she could control it. "I cannot accept anything more from her ladyship."

What she wanted was not jewelry, but something to cover this embarrassing display of bosom. However, given the fact that she was already mortified to be wearing something belonging to a lady with whom she was not even acquainted, she decided near nudity was preferable to begging further favors.

Ten minutes later she made her way down the grand staircase that ended at the vestibule, and with some trepidation she followed a footman to the door of the blue withdrawing room, where the family was to meet before the guests arrived. After knocking discretely, the footman opened the door, announced her to the lady already there, then stepped aside, leaving Delia exposed to the rigorously polite smile affixed to Lady Regina's face.

Lady Regina was a most attractive woman. Sixtyish, but with the figure and carriage of a much younger woman, she was beautifully dressed and coiffed. Her salmon-colored sarcenet, like the bronze she lent Delia, was simple yet elegant. An India silk wrap was draped artfully across her shoulders, and around her throat was fastened a double rope of pearls that added just the perfect finish to her ensemble.

Delia curtsied politely. Then, while mentally labeling herself a fool for not insisting upon a tray in her room, she waited to see what Mitchell's mother would do. Etiquette dictated that her ladyship be allowed to speak first.

"Miss Eskew," she said with a decided touch of frost in her voice, "how do you do?"

So, the line had been drawn!

Delia's spine straightened just that extra fraction, and her chin lifted perceptibly. She could understand Lady Regina's reserve; after all, her son had brought a Gypsy into his home—and a bedraggled one at that. Under the circumstances, Delia was willing to be as conciliatory as necessary. However, if anyone—and she meant *anyone*—thought to make her feel that she was out of her element, they would need to think again.

She was a gentleman's daughter, and she hoped she knew how to conduct herself in society. She was not Paulie Diggs, awed by being in the presence of his betters, nor was she some inexperienced chit to be intimidated by a cool tone and a less-than convivial reception.

"I am well, thank you, Lady Regina. I hope my unexpected arrival has not upset your numbers at table. And, lest I forget to mention it later, I thank you most sincerely for the loan of this beautiful dress.

I shall endeavor to return it to you without reminders of my having worn it."

Lady Regina was caught off guard by the speech—by the confident utterance of it as well as by the fact that the young woman spoke in an educated manner. Furthermore, from the spark of challenge in those topaz eyes, it would appear the Gypsy did not think undue deference necessary. A very smart tactic, actually, for Lady Regina detested a toady. Intrigued, she unbent so far as to offer her hand for shaking.

The young woman came forward, held the proffered hand for the minimum of seconds, then released it. "Pray allow me," she said, "to offer my condolences on the recent loss of your nephew, Mr. William Holcomb. He was a fine gentleman."

As before, she spoke without the least shyness, a fact that made Lady Regina wonder just what sort of Gypsy her son had stumbled on to. "You were acquainted with my nephew?"

"Only for a matter of months. Long enough, however, to state without reservation that he will be missed by all those who knew him."

Regina felt unwanted moisture in her eyes, for she had known William from the moment of his birth, and she had always had a soft spot in her heart for him. He was her nephew by marriage, rather than blood, but he was such a dear, thoughtful boy that she had taken almost as much pride in his accomplishments as she did in those of her own son. Actually, William and his Uncle Conrad were in many ways closer than Conrad and Mitchell, for uncle and nephew held many of the same political views.

They were forever discussing ways to make the government run more smoothly, not to mention work more equably for the poor laborers whose employment was disappearing as a result of the installation of modern machinery. In fact, the very day before

William's murder, he and Conrad had been closeted together for the better part of the afternoon, their discussion so private her husband had locked the door to his book room and given word that he and William were not to be disturbed.

Recalling the seriousness of her nephew's young face the last time she saw him, Regina felt the tears spill from her eyes to train down her cheeks. Sorry to have exhibited such personal emotion before a stranger, she turned her head and dabbed at the moisture with a dainty square of linen.

"Forgive me," the Gypsy said. "I did not mean to cause you discomfort."

The regret in her voice was so genuine, the warmth in those brown eyes so sincere, that Regina forgot entirely that she wished to remain aloof from this stranger her son had brought with him from Ems Regis. "Think nothing of it, my dear. It is as you say, William was a fine gentleman, and he will be missed."

She wanted to ask how someone who lived on the West Sussex coast came to meet her nephew, who spent most of his days in town, but before she could do more than take a breath, the door was opened and Mitchell entered the room. As always, her heart filled with pride at the sight of her son.

Just being able to look at him was a treat for her, for she had missed him dreadfully while he served in the Peninsula. Naturally, she had feared for his safety each and every day, and she had thanked heaven when he returned to them alive and in one piece. Still strong. Still handsome.

He looked especially attractive this evening, dressed in burgundy-colored evening clothes that proclaimed him every inch the gentleman, and a pearl waistcoat with silver stripes that called attention to his gray eyes. He was so tall and so full of life, and just the sort of brave, good-hearted man to make any mother proud.

Of course, Conrad was proud of him as well. Though when it came to sons, fathers had a way of ranking honor and intelligence above a kind heart.

"Mother," Mitchell said, lifting her hand to his lips. "May I say how elegant you look this evening?"

Before she could reply, he turned to his guest and bowed over her hand, though he did not bring it to his lips. "Dee," he said, "I am pleased you decided to join us."

He said nothing of how lovely the bronze silk looked against the young woman's ivory skin, nor how becomingly her hair had been arranged, with the drifting tendrils emphasizing her pretty cheekbones and the delicate curve of her jaw. But from the way his eyes took in every inch of her, from her head down to her toes, apparently without missing a single detail of her attire or the figure beneath, Regina decided that what her son *did not* say was far more significant than what he actually said. For Dee Eskew there was none of the casual flattery he might have paid any other young female who was a guest in his home.

Not for nothing was Regina married to a member of Parliament, a man who was obliged to keep safe many of the secrets of government. For thirty-five years she had observed Conrad Holcomb, and she knew without question when he was considering something important, something he could not share with her.

It was the same with her son. He had something on his mind, but it was something he had no intention of sharing, least of all with his mother. Of only one thing was she certain. Whatever his thoughts, Miss Dee Eskew, Gypsy, was at their core. And for that reason, Regina was resolved to watch the young woman very carefully. Very carefully indeed.

Lady Regina Holcomb had learned years ago not to interfere in things that were none of her concern, and by following the dictates of practical, good sense, she had proven herself an excellent wife for a politician. Good mothers, she felt sure, would do well to embrace similar courses of action, so from the outset she had decided to say little and to allow her son to introduce his guest in whatever manner he saw fit. The results would be on his head.

When the first of the dinner guests arrived, however, Regina surrendered to a charitable impulse and introduced Dee Eskew as a friend of hers, thereby insuring the young woman's immediate acceptance. She did not elaborate on the nature of their acquaintance, merely allowed everyone to assume that Dee had come to Fernbourne with her. Gypsy or not, the chit was a guest in her son's house, and Regina could not allow her to be given the cut direct, an act that would certainly happen if it was discovered she had traveled alone with Mitchell.

The fabrication brought unexpected rewards, for Mitchell, disregarding the interested stares of his neighbors, bent down and kissed his mother's cheek. "Nine years," he said, "is too long to be away. It allows a fellow to forget all the things he most admires in his lady mother."

Regina said nothing. How could she, with her heart in her throat, blocking all speech. Fortunately, more guests were announced and she was obliged to resume her post as hostess. Even so, her son's compliment warmed her throughout the evening.

As it turned out, only twelve guests sat down to dinner. Lady Yarborough and her cousin, the guest of honor, were unavoidably detained, though they sent word that they would arrive in plenty of time for cards.

Even with the last-minute removal of the two chairs, and the quick rearranging of place settings, the dinner went well. The food was deliciously prepared and the wine sat gently on the palate. Furthermore, the conversation was lively enough to suit any hostess.

During the meal, Lady Regina studied Dee Eskew every chance she got, but she could detect nothing in the Gypsy's speech or deportment that would reveal her low birth. Despite what Mitchell had said earlier, the chit did not eat with her fingers. In fact, her table manners were impeccable. As well, she conversed easily with her dinner partners, never once betraying a lack of social graces.

Once the sweet was eaten—an apricot blancmange with almonds—the ladies left the gentlemen to their port and made their way to the red withdrawing room, where four baize-covered games tables had been set up. To Regina's relief, Dee Eskew said she had no wish to play. Gypsies were reputed to know all manner of tricks with cards, and since a private party was no place to display such talents, Regina was pleased to accept her refusal.

"You are quite certain?"

"Quite certain, ma'am. I am an indifferent player at best, so unless you need someone to make up the numbers at one of the tables, I should prefer to sit beside that lovely fire."

Suiting the action to the words, she carried a petit-point tuffet over to a red damask wing chair occupied by Mrs. Fitz-James, an elderly neighbor who had spent the better part of the dinner boring her companions by cataloging the many attributes of her newest great-grandson. "May I join you, Mrs. Fitz-James?"

"Please do, my dear. I daresay you are the only one of the guests who would come near me, for I fear I have been prosing on like one demented."

"Not at all, ma'am. Besides, I have a soft spot in my heart for infants."

At the elderly lady's smile, Dee Eskew said, "I do not remember, ma'am, if you mentioned the little boy's age."

Mrs. Fitz-James brightened immediately, and it was not to be wondered at when her reply became a soliloquy. "Simon is not yet a year old, my dear. And though you will say I have a partiality, I must tell you that he is the most beautiful child I have ever seen. Should you ever see him, I am persuaded you would agree."

"I am sure I should, ma'am. Have you a miniature of the lad?"

As Mrs. Fitz-James began to dig into her overflowing reticule for the miniature, Lady Regina left the pair. Even as she moved away, she wondered about Dee Eskew. Was she the thoughtful, pretty, behaved young woman she appeared, or was she merely a consummate actress out to fool them all into complacency?

Like any good hostess, Regina circled the room, speaking with each of the ladies in turn, and checking the four gaming tables to assure herself that the seals were unbroken on the packs of cards and that gaming chips and score sheets were at hand if needed. Two of the ladies were already seated at their chosen table, and the third stood beside a chair, waiting for her hostess to join her for cribbage. "Please," she said, "be seated. I will return in a moment."

Having completed the circle, Regina arrived near enough to Mrs. Fitz-James to hear her conclude a story that bore all the signs of having been long and rather involved. "You must forgive an old lady, my dear," she said at last. "It is just that I am so proud of the boy."

Dee Eskew's smile appeared sincere. "You have every reason to be proud, ma'am. I know only a little about young children, but I believe it is rare for a male infant to form sentences at such an early age. Your great-grandson must be quite intelligent."

"Oh, he is. He is."

Without drawing a breath, Mrs. Fitz-James called to Regina. "Dear Lady Regina," she said, "where did you meet this delightful young lady?"

Delia held her breath, waiting to hear what her hostess would say. Would she tell a second fib? Or would she admit that her "guest" had been unknown to her until two hours ago?

As it happened, the lady was required to do neither, for the gentlemen chose that moment to enter the room. They had not remained long at their port, and in the stir their entry caused, Delia excused herself to Mrs. Fitz-James and crossed over to a tall window that faced onto the carriageway.

It would be dark soon, and the servants would close the red-and-gold-striped brocade drapery against the evening chill. For the moment, however, Delia stood in the embrasure, enjoying the muted pinks and oranges that swept the western sky. Twilight had cast its magic upon the lawn, turning it a lush dark green, and she was imagining how pretty the walled garden beyond would look in the moonlight, when she felt someone standing behind her.

Even without turning, she knew it was Mitchell Holcomb. Something about the man—confidence, perhaps, or simply male vitality—seemed to emanate from him, and she felt the force of it against her back as surely as she had felt the warmth of his body the night before when they had slept in the Diggs's barn.

To her chagrin, she found herself remembering her response to the feel of their bodies touching so intimately. Not wanting to recall the rest of the embarrassing experience, she began to whistle softly. Only when Mitchell chuckled did she realize the title of the song that had come unbidden to her pursed lips. It was "My Darling, Gray-Eyed Soldier."

Drat! Why that of all songs?

"Have you a darling, gray-eyed soldier?" he asked. The words were a mere whisper spoken very close to her ear, and his voice was so warm it left her feeling quite nerveless.

"No. No, I have not."

"Would you like one?"

Delia knew he was teasing her. Unfortunately, her heart was not so perceptive, and that foolish organ accelerated most uncomfortably, as if he had made the offer for real. "No, Major, I would not like a soldier of any sort."

"Too bad," he said. "As it happens, I know where there is one going for half the regular price."

Her breath caught in her throat. He was teasing, she reminded herself, and she was not some dewy-eyed girl easily led astray by a handsome face and a charming manner. She was twenty-eight years old—a sensible woman—and as such it behooved her to keep her head.

Adopting what she hoped would pass for a bright tone, she said, "Sorry, Major, but my pockets are to let, as the saying goes."

"A pity," he said.

Was there just a touch of regret in his voice?

Wanting to know if she had imagined it, Delia turned, and when she did, she looked directly into Mitchell's eyes. In the fading light, those gray orbs were shadowed, their expression hidden. All that was clearly revealed was the sharpness of his chin with its hint of a cleft.

He was standing very close to her. Much too close. And his nearness made her feel warm all over.

Drat the man! Why could he not step back and give her room? Surely he must know that his nearness made her uncomfortable.

He knew! The smile that tugged at the corners of his firm, well-shaped lips gave him away.

Angry with him for making sport of her, and with herself for reacting like some silly, schoolroom miss, she put her hand on his chest and gave him a slight shove.

It was a mistake. He did not budge, and the feel of his rock-hard chest beneath her palm and outstretched

fingers gave her a decidedly lethargic feeling, one that
bade her lean toward him so he could take her weight
against his powerful, unyielding body.

Foolish, foolish woman! Had she no shame?

The seconds passed, and Delia did not realize that
she was still touching Mitchell's chest until he reached
up and covered her hand with his own. His fingers
were strong as they clasped hers, and the warmth of
his touch seemed to flow up her arm and through her
body, infusing every part of her with an awareness
that was at once mesmerizing and exhilarating.

"You . . . you should move away," she said.

"Should I?" he asked softly. "And why is that?"

"Why?"

She could not think why. All she knew for certain
was that his closeness was having a hypnotic effect upon
her, and that he smelled wonderfully masculine—a
blend of sandalwood shaving soap and good, clean,
male. Left to her own devices, Delia would have
leaned close enough to fill her nostrils, and— And
embarrass them both in the process!

Her lips felt dry, and when she licked them with
the tip of her tongue, Mitchell drew in a sharp breath.
"Dee, I—"

Fortunately for Delia's sanity, their disturbing tête-
à-tête was interrupted by the sudden opening of the
withdrawing room door. Lady Yarborough and her
cousin had arrived at last, and as the footman announced them, Mitchell put his hand beneath Delia's
elbow and led her forward to help him greet the
latecomers.

"Lady Yarborough," he said. He bowed to the
hawk-nosed, arrogant-looking lady, and in response
she inclined her turbaned head just the least bit. "So
nice of you to come, ma'am."

"Nonsense, Holcomb. Sorry we were detained. But
never mind, for we are here now. Make your bow to
my cousin, Lord Leeland. Thomas, this is our host,

Major Mitchell Holcomb, whom I have known since he was a lad in leading strings."

The two men bowed. "Your servant," Mitchell said.

"And yourth, thir."

Even though lisps were all the rage among the *ton*, Mitchell stared at the simpering, middle-aged fop, distaste for the affectation written plainly upon his unsmiling face.

As for Delia, she stood frozen to the spot, her gaze riveted to the slender gentleman whose still blond hair was carefully combed into a Brutus. His evening clothes—a masterpiece in puce satin—were complemented by rhinestone shoe buckles and a cravat pin whose diamond was the size of a plumped currant. But it was neither his attire nor his affected speech that held her captive as a hare caught in a hunter's aim. It was the man himself.

"Upon my word!" he said, raising his quizzing glass to his eye, the better to examine her. "It ith you!"

Mitchell looked from the gentleman to Delia, a question in his glance. When Delia said nothing—could say nothing for the obstruction in her throat—Mitchell began the introductions. "Lady Yarborough. Lord Leeland. May I introduce my guest, Miss Dee—"

"No need to introduth me," the gentleman in puce said, "for the young lady and I are old acquaintanthes."

Unable to look at Mitchell, Delia curtsied to Lady Yarborough. "Ma'am," she said.

Her ladyship demanded to know how her cousin knew the young lady. "Tell me at once," she ordered, "for I cannot abide being left in the dark about these things."

"Yes," Mitchell said, his tone coldly polite, "enlighten us, my lord, for it seems that I, too, am in the dark."

"It ith thertainly no mythtery," his lordship replied, "for I have known the young lady anytime theth ten yearth. Even before my dear friend, Lord Sheffield, married her mother.''

Delia snuck a quick look at Mitchell, whose expression was a mixture of bewilderment and incredulity. "Lord Sheffield," he repeated.

"My, yeth," the fop replied. He turned the full force of his simpering manner on Delia. "Ith that not true, Mith Barrington?"

Chapter Twelve

*T*he hour that followed was sheer torment for Delia. Lord Leeland seemed eager to speak with her of old friends they shared in London, while Mitchell appeared disinclined to speak to her at all. Nor even to look at her, for that matter. He played the perfect host, smiling and making certain the latecomers found games to their liking, but not once did he bestow that smile or those well-bred manners upon Delia.

Finally, after the tea tray had been brought in, and she had forced a few sips of the steaming brew past her taut lips, Delia excused herself and went directly to her bedchamber. With the maid's assistance, she removed the bronze-colored creation and donned the utilitarian night rail and the ugly mustard-colored flannel dressing gown lent her by Mrs. Newly. Knowing she was too emotionally distraught to sleep, she asked Betty to build up the fire. When the fire crackled invitingly and the screen was in place, Delia pulled a buttercup-yellow slipper chair close to the hearth.

"Will that be all, miss?"

"Yes, thank you, Betty. Please be so kind as to take the dinner dress with you. Sponge and press it first thing tomorrow, and return it to Lady Regina's woman, with my appreciation."

"Yes, miss." Her tasks completed, the maid curtsied, then wished Delia a pleasant night.

As soon as the door clicked shut and she was alone, Delia hid her face in her hands. Regrettably, the comfort of tears was denied her. She had lied, and the lies had caught up with her. Was this, then, the fate of all liars? This hollow feeling in the region of the heart? Was this pain of regret the price she was to pay for having delayed too long in telling the truth?

Earlier that day she had made a silent vow to lay the whole story before Mitchell tomorrow. As it happened, fate had other plans, and Delia had been exposed before she could explain the circumstances that led her to conceal her true identity.

If she had told him herself, he might have understood her fear and forgiven her for misleading him. But not now. Now he would believe that she had confessed the truth only because she had been caught in a falsehood.

She had not bothered to braid her loosened hair, and now she ran her hands through it as if hoping to relieve the pressure inside her brain. When that failed, she leaned her head back against the top of the comfortably upholstered chair and stretched her slippered feet toward the fire screen.

Considering the trials she had been put through the day before, combined with the warmth of the fire, Delia should have fallen asleep. She did not. In fact, she sat there for what felt like hours, wide awake and staring into the fire, watching the dancing of the blue-and-orange flames with a devotion they had done nothing to deserve.

The yellow bedchamber was at the front of the house, so she knew when Lady Regina's party began to break up. She heard the various conveyances being called for, then the rattle of the carriage wheels as those vehicles traveled down the crushed-stone carriageway to the wrought-iron gates and beyond. Finally, the last guest was sent on his way, the bolt on the front door was shot home, and the house and its occupants settled down for the night.

All was quiet save the tall case clock at the end of the corridor. Delia counted as the venerable timepiece *bonged* twelve times. The deep, resonant sounds still echoed in her head when she heard a soft tapping at her bedchamber door.

"Who . . . who is it?"

The question was unnecessary, for even though the person on the other side of the door made no reply, Delia knew without a doubt that it was Mitchell who stood in the darkened corridor. Just as she knew he would be furious with her.

The fire had burned itself to little more than embers, but they gave enough light for her to see to cross the carpet to the door. When she opened it, Mitchell stood there, a single pewter candlestick in his hand, the flickering of the candle flame causing eerie shapes to dance upon the corridor ceiling.

He was still fully dressed, but he had loosened his cravat and unbuttoned his waistcoat. His black hair was rumpled, as though he had run his fingers through it, but even *en deshabille* he was still the handsomest man Delia had ever seen. Handsome and enraged.

"Well?" he said, the sharpness of the word giving further indication of his anger. "Do we talk here, where anyone might hear, or may I come inside?"

"Come in," she replied.

Lifting the hem of the ugly dressing gown, Delia stepped back, giving Mitchell ample room to pass her. Once he was inside the bedchamber—a room she had thought of as quite large—it seemed to shrink, making her feel as though she could not move about for fear of bumping into him.

Without asking permission, Mitchell went to the fireplace, set his candle on the mantelpiece, then fed several shovelfuls of coal onto the embers. By the time

Delia had resumed her seat, the fire was beginning to come to life.

"If you wish to sit," she said, "there is a stool at the dressing table."

"A bit late to be playing the perfect hostess," he said. Ignoring her offer of the stool, he propped his shoulder against the mantel. "I prefer my truth straight up. That is, if you know how to tell the truth, Miss Barrington."

The way he said her name, it was accusation, trial, and conviction all in one.

Delia was unsure where to start. An apology, perhaps? "You have reason to be angry with me, I suppose, but—"

"Excuse me! You *suppose* I have reason to be angry? You suppose! Madam, I would be justified in throttling you! I have been drugged, bludgeoned, and shot at by people I do not even know. And," he added, rubbing his chin, "you even had a go at me yourself."

"I apologized for that!"

He ignored her outburst. "After the ordeals I have been put through on your account, no court in the land would convict me of murder."

Delia knew he would not murder her, nor even lay hands on her, but her mouth went dry as flannel at the suppressed fury in his voice. "I had planned to tell you everything tomorrow. Though I daresay you will not believe me."

He laughed, but the sound held no humor. "Believe you? Madam, I would as soon trust the most hardened criminal in Newgate."

Apparently unable to remain still another minute, he strode over to the window, then turned as soon as he reached the embrasure and walked back to the hearth. "Answer me this," he said, his hands balled into fists, but held motionless beside his long, powerful legs. "Are you a congenital liar, or were these entire two days staged for my benefit, to keep me from my purpose in traveling to Ems Regis?''

She would have liked to disclaim any responsibility for the events of the past two days, but honesty compelled her to admit that none of it would have occurred except for her. That she had wanted none of it to happen was beside the point. "I meant only to protect Robbie."

"From me?" His tone was incredulous. "What maggot got inside your brain that you supposed me the sort of man who would harm a child?"

She had no answer, and when she did not reply, he swore. "Deuce take it, madam! Do you think it still?"

Delia shook her head. "No, no. Of course not. Not now. But when you first arrived at Sky Cottage, I knew nothing about you, save that you were heir presumptive to Sir Allistair's title and lands. I was unaware of your personal situation . . . of this beautiful estate and the fact that you are the grandson of an earl."

"How remiss of me to have failed to enlighten you upon our first meeting, Miss Barrington. The next time I respond to a letter from a complete stranger—one I had every reason to suspect might be some sort of extortionist—I will be certain to brag about my home and my connections at every opportunity."

Delia felt her back stiffen. "There is no need for sarcasm, sir. By your own admission you suspected my motives. Can you not understand that I would suspect yours?"

"But why should you? *I* did not lie about my name. *I* made no secret of who I was, or that I had come in answer to the letter."

"True enough, but your name was all I knew of you, nothing else. For all I knew, you were a half-pay officer living on the expectations of your uncle's wealth. Poverty is a most compelling force. Was I to trust that you would not consider William's son and

heir an inconvenience? An inconvenience best elimi-
nated as soon as possible?"

She was obliged to clear her throat, for she found
her next remark very difficult to utter. "I had already
witnessed the murder of your cousin. I was helpless
to do anything to save William, but I was resolved to
keep his son safe at all costs. I could not stand by and
see my sweet Robbie endangered."

Mitchell heard the huskiness in her voice, and at
the sound, the anger in him seemed to dissipate like
fog before the sun. She had meant only to protect the
child. And however misguided her judgment, it had
been influenced by the cruel reality of William's death.
She had witnessed the murder, and that could not
have been easy for her.

In his nine years of soldiering, Mitchell had seen
many a grown man after his first brush with violent
death, retching at the side of the road, his face pale
as a lily, his eyes dull with shock. Could he forgive a
career soldier his momentary weakness, yet expect
more from a gently reared female? Especially one
whose only objective was to protect a little boy.

"Is the lad truly William's son?"

Her attention had been focused on her hands, where
they lay in her lap. Her fingers were entwined in what
was probably a painful grip, and her unbound hair had
fallen forward like a silk curtain, concealing most of
her face. When he spoke, however, she pushed the
hair aside and looked up, hope and disbelief mingling
in her expression.

"Robbie? Oh, yes. It is as I wrote in my letter.
Your cousin and Maria Eskew were married secretly.
I believe the reason for the secrecy had something to
do with Sir Allistair's dream of a much more advanta-
geous alliance."

Mitchell knew of his uncle's dreams for his only son,
they had their basis in the fact that Conrad Holcomb,
Sir Allistair's young brother, had married the daughter

of an earl. Still, Sir Allistair was no ogre. He loved his son, and given time to adjust to the idea, he would not have rejected the woman to whom William had given his heart and his hand.

"The child is unquestionably a Holcomb," Delia said. "Back at Sky Cottage, I have the papers to prove what I say."

"Then it would appear that we have no recourse but to return to the cottage. For the papers, and for young Robbie."

"For Robbie? Then you believe me?"

At his nod, she rose from the slipper chair, as if unable to remain still another moment. "You may find this difficult to believe, sir, but lying does not come easily to me. With all my heart, I wish I had not felt the need to resort to subterfuge. But in all honesty, Mitchell . . . I mean, Major, I—"

"Please, call me Mitchell."

It was an olive branch, and she must have recognized it as such. "Mitchell," she whispered.

She sighed loudly, and with the expulsion of breath her entire body seemed to relax. The relief in her face was enough to make any red-blooded man want to take her in his arms and assure her that all would be well. Mitchell did not do so, of course, for at that hour and in this place, it would have been more than his red blood could withstand!

Considering all the emotional chaos he had endured these past few hours, to touch her would have proven disastrous. Especially with her wearing nothing more than a nightrail and that ridiculous dressing gown. He was already fighting an almost uncontrollable urge to run his fingers through the silken lengths of her hair. Not that the urge ended there; far from it, for he positively ached to lift her in his arms and carry her over to that most inviting-looking bed.

For both their sakes, he hoped she could not read his mind.

"Mitchell," she said again, and his name on her lips was a caress to his ears. "You are a good man."

If she could say that, it was obvious she could not read his thoughts!

"But I wonder," she continued, "if that goodness will extend far enough to allow you to forgive me. I am truly sorry for having lied to you, and I hope that someday you will trust me again."

Moisture pooled in those lovely topaz eyes, and her bottom lip trembled just the least little bit before she caught it between her teeth. Her struggle not to cry was sorely testing Mitchell's resolve to remember that he was a gentleman, and he knew that if he did not get out of her bedchamber in the next few seconds, there would be the devil to pay.

"I trust you," he said.

"And the other?" She looked up at him with such pleading in her eyes that only a man made of stone could have refused her.

"And I forgive you."

Recalling that she had once said those words to him, when he had begged to be forgiven for having thrown her in the moat, he made a fist and tapped her very lightly on her chin. "But never do that again."

Her laugh was a watery gurgle that all but robbed him of his senses. "I promise," she said. "And thank you for not repaying me in kind."

He took a step closer to her, so that mere inches separated them. "Since you are not, in fact, Dee Eskew, what do I call you? Considering all that has passed between us, I think Miss Barrington a bit formal."

"Quite formal," she said, the words spoken softly. "If you wish to do so, you may call me Cordelia. Or, you may do as my friends do, and call me Delia."

Mitchell dared not repeat her name. In the magic of the firelight, to utter it would have been much too intimate. Even so, he felt justified in collecting at least a token compensation for his troubles, so he put his finger beneath her chin and lifted it. With her face turned up to his, he bent slowly and brushed his lips against hers.

The temptation to linger there, with his mouth upon her sweet mouth, was almost overwhelming. Though he longed to pull her hard against him and feel her respond to his kiss, he released her while he still could and strode to the door. "Tomorrow," he said, his hand on the latch, "we have much to discuss."

"Tomorrow," she repeated, the word a bit breathless.

"Good night," he said.

Before she could reply, he turned and exited the room, closing the door softly behind him. Only when he reached the far end of the corridor did his breathing return to normal.

Chapter Thirteen

Delia slept the sleep of the forgiven sinner, and when she awoke the next morning, feeling wonderfully refreshed, the maid was opening the window hangings. "Good morning, Betty."

"Good morning to you, miss. It's a beautiful day out. The rain's all gone, and we've nothing but sunshine and songbirds." She pointed to the polished teak tray she had set on the dressing table. "There's a pot of chocolate beneath the cozy, and some currant buns just out of the oven. And a note. You want I should bring the tray to the bed?"

"Just the note, thank you."

Delia stretched lazily, then sat up and plumped the pillows behind her, the better to read the folded paper. As she had suspected, the missive was from Mitchell, and at her first glimpse of his penmanship, she smiled. His handwriting was like the man himself—large, honest, and without frills.

> Delia,
> I must speak with one of my tenants first thing this morning, but I should return around ten. Will you meet me in the garden?
>
> Mitchell

Remembering his parting remark last evening, that

they had much to discuss, Delia could guess why he wanted to meet in the garden. They would have privacy there, and they could remain as long as they wished without offending the proprieties, or Mitchell's mother. By now, Lady Regina would have been informed about Delia's real name and social status, and no matter how calmly her ladyship may have received that news, chances were she would be displeased to discover that her son and his guest were alone for more than a few minutes behind closed doors.

Actually, the idea of a short walk in the sunshine suited Delia perfectly. The last thing she wanted to do was sit in one of the formal withdrawing rooms dressed in her Gypsy clothes and her one shoe. That is, if her clothes had been returned to her. When she last saw the filthy, odoriferous garments, Mrs. Newly had given orders that they be taken to the scullery and soaked overnight in lye water.

"Betty?"

"Yes, miss?"

"I need my clothes. Do you know what happened to them?"

In answer to the question, the maid crossed the room to the walnut clothespress, where she removed the blue skirt and cream bodice. "Here they be, miss, all freshly washed and ironed."

Carrying them as respectfully as she might have done expensive silks, she laid the cotton garments across the slipper chair. "And if you'll not be offended, miss, I've brought you my Sunday boots and stockings, and Mrs. Newly sent along the shawl the master give her last boxing day. I held the boots up to your old one, and they look a match. I think they'll do."

Delia was almost undone by the servants' generosity, and she was obliged to blink back the sudden tears that stung her eyes. Making a mental note to return the items, along with appropriate gifts, she thanked the maid and asked her to express her appreciation to the housekeeper.

After breaking her fast with one of the currant buns and a cup of perfectly sweetened chocolate topped with a dollop of cream, Delia pulled on the unembroidered white stockings and the jean half boots, which fit her perfectly. When she donned the skirt and bodice, she could not determine which pleased her most, the clean, fresh smell of the garments, or the fact that they were hers—or almost hers.

She tossed the paisley shawl around her shoulders, in case the sun should decide to play hide-and-seek, then hurried down the corridor and out the front entrance. Continuing to the walled garden, she kept to the crushed-stone footpath to avoid getting Betty's boots wet in the still dewy grass.

The garden was a charming retreat, where rows of pink-tinged stepping stones serpentined around various planting beds of flowers and herbs, the focal point of each bed some sort of blossoming fruit tree. After pausing for a moment to enjoy a veritable blanket of blue and purple pansies, Delia continued toward a pretty arched trellis. A wooden bench had been placed beneath the trellis, and while Delia sat there, enjoying the beauty of the May morning, she heard the rich, clear song of a skylark.

The little yellowish-brown bird was at the far end of the garden, perched on the branch of a small apricot tree that had been espaliered to encourage it to grow flat against the wall. Almost as soon as Delia spied the little fellow, something startled him and he ceased singing and took flight.

Delia thought she heard footsteps, but when she called out and no one answered, she decided she must have been mistaken. Not that it mattered, for at just that moment she saw Mitchell gallop up the carriageway on a handsome, spirited roan. At the sight of him, she felt her heart accelerate its beating, and not wanting to play the shy maiden, she left the bench and went to wait for him beside the garden entrance.

Dressed in a Prussian blue riding coat and slate gray pantaloons, he looked truly splendid astride the large animal, like the fearless warrior he was. He saw Delia right away, and while the stable lad took charge of the roan, Mitchell hurried across the lawn toward her, obviously not caring in the least that his black Hessians would be covered with dew.

"You are here," he said, a smile softening the hard contours of his face. "I had hoped you would be."

Though not at all displeased to hear the happiness in his voice, she refrained from telling him that she came almost the moment she read his note. No point in flattering him by admitting her eagerness to be in his company. Especially not if what Betty said about him was true, that he was much sought after by the marriageable ladies of the *ton*.

Suddenly struck by the truth of the servant's observation, Delia felt a blush warm her cheeks.

Mitchell Holcomb was rich, handsome, and well connected—a *premier parti*. As such, he would be a prime target for the match-making mamas, and chances were he could have his pick of the pretty girls swelling the ranks at Almack's. Chits fresh from the schoolroom, and as yet unspoiled by the adversities of life. Girls ready to sit adoringly at the feet of a military hero.

Young girls. Not some twenty-eight-year-old spinster who had not seen the inside of Almack's in more than two years. Though no ape-leader, Delia knew that a woman of her age was considered on the shelf, and she was realistic enough not to mistake Mitchell's friendly greeting for a declaration of love.

Love! When had that idea reared its head?

How absurd? Foolish beyond permission! She was not in love with Mitchell Holcomb.

Or was she?

No! Definitely not. Most emphatically not. They were complete opposites.

Delia knew who and what she was; she had had days, months, years to consider the subject. She was a loyal friend and a loyal family member—or she would be if she had any family. She needed love and romance, but she also needed steadfastness. Everyone she had ever loved had left her, and she needed to know that the man to whom she gave her heart would not desert her.

The last thing she wanted was adventure, and Mitchell Holcomb was first and foremost an adventurer.

He was a warrior, and like the Vikings of old—those fearless, virile men who sailed away in search of worlds unknown—love and home would never take first place in his heart. He would never want or need her as much as she needed and wanted him.

She wanted him! As breathless as that thought left her, it was true. She wanted Mitchell Holcomb, and she wanted him to want her, and that just proved what a fool she was. Only a fool would want a man she could never have.

And even if she got him, it would only be temporary. Soon he would tire of domesticity and be off on another adventure, leaving her with a broken heart.

Foolish, foolish woman, to entertain even the idea of loving such a man.

The warmth in her cheeks turned to fire, and for a moment Delia thought she would be consumed by the raging heat. Her heart beat as though she had just climbed a mountain, and she felt as though her tongue had been tied in knots, rendering her incapable of speech. But she must speak, and soon. Mitchell had said how pleased he was that she was here in the garden, waiting for him, and now he was smiling at her, waiting for her reply.

Using all her mental reserves, she willed herself to be calm, so he did not guess her foolish thoughts.

For the first time in their acquaintance, Delia felt ill at ease in his presence, and for that reason she greeted him with more coolness than she had intended. "Good morning," she said, her tone very nearly frosty enough to cause the pansies to close in on themselves.

For his part, Mitchell was disappointed by her cool greeting. Was this her way of putting distance between them?

Over the past two days, circumstances had obliged them to be in company with one another—more intimate company that was considered proper. In some ways, he had been glad of the forced intimacy, for it had moved their friendship well past the strict formality required of a man and woman of their class.

Had he been alone in his feelings? Perhaps Miss Cordelia Barrington would prefer that they embrace a more formal relationship.

He knew nothing of Cordelia Barrington. As the stepdaughter of Lord Sheffield, she was a stranger to Mitchell. She was no longer Dee Eskew, and without the Gypsy mask to conceal her true identity, perhaps everything was now changed.

Where was Dee Eskew? Where was his Dee? The brave, wonderful woman he had come to know. The woman who had slept in his arms, with only a blanket separating her naked body from his.

Last night, after he left her bedchamber, Mitchell had spent the better part of the night aching for her. He had wanted her as he had never wanted a woman in his entire life. Remembering the way she had looked in the firelight, with her skin all glowing and warm, and her glorious hair falling about her shoulders, he had imagined himself removing that ridiculous dressing gown and kissing every inch of her lovely body.

Just before he left her bedchamber, he had kissed her and had longed to pull her hard against him and feel her response to his kiss. Could it be that this coolness *was* her response? Was this Miss Cordelia Barrington's subtle way of telling him that she wanted none of him or his kisses?

As if in answer to his unspoken questions, she turned and began to walk toward the bottom of the garden, her boots tapping softly on the stepping stones. Immediately she began to speak of Maria Eskew, as if to imply that her sole purpose in meeting him was to have that discussion he mentioned last night before quitting her bedchamber.

Mitchell swore beneath his breath. He had thought Delia was as attracted to him as he was to her. Obviously he had been wrong.

Though the idea hit him in the chest like a well-aimed punch, he managed to keep his feelings from showing on his face. No point in making her afraid to be around him. If formality was what she wanted, formality was what she would get.

Never a man to force his attentions upon a woman, he fell into step with her and took up the conversation, though he missed the first part of what she was saying. ". . . that same year, she and I entered Miss Plemshaw's Female Academy."

She? Was Delia still talking about Maria Eskew? "Nadja Eskew's granddaughter was at school with you? A Gypsy? At a female academy?"

"I doubt Miss Plemshaw ever knew of Maria's connection to the Romany people."

"Even so, how was such schooling possible? The expense alone—"

"As I said before, Nadja's daughter married the son of a wealthy banker."

So, that was what he had missed earlier. Admonishing himself to pay attention, he bid her continue.

"Like me, Maria grew up in London. That was what

first brought us together, our homesickness for London—homesickness and the fact that we had both lost our fathers. Though she was a cit's daughter, and my stepfather was Lord Sheffield, we became friends. We were inseparable at school, and we continued our friendship afterward. Though, of course, we traveled in much different social circles."

"I suppose she coaxed you into inviting her to *ton* parties, and that was how she met my unsuspecting cousin."

Delia stared at him as if surprised by the question. "You are very quick to judge, sir. Neither Maria nor William deserve such vilification."

Mitchell took the rebuke without rancor. The chit was Delia's friend, and even now she would not hear anything against her. "I beg your pardon," he said. "And theirs."

Apparently placated, Delia continued. "Maria was not a social climber. She was quite well liked in her own circle, and she had no desire to quit the sphere in which she was most comfortable."

"Then how did she and William meet?"

"By accident. Literally. At least once a week, Maria and I spent an afternoon together, visiting in one another's homes or enjoying the delights of town . . . museum, lectures, that sort of thing. It was during one such excursion, while we were viewing the Elgin Marbles, that I accidentally stepped on a gentleman's foot."

"Allow me to guess. That gentleman was my cousin."

She nodded. "I knew William Holcomb slightly, for we had stood up together more than once at private parties. For that reason, I thought nothing of exchanging a few pleasantries with him."

She smiled, as if remembering the incident with fondness. "As it happened, he was there alone. And since he had had the foresight to purchase a program, and I had not, I invited him to join us and tell us which of the friezes and sculptures we should most admire."

"And he did so?"

"With apparent pleasure. We shared a most enjoyable hour viewing the marbles, and later, when William asked if he might treat us to ices at Gunter's, I saw no reason to refuse the invitation. Before the afternoon was gone, it was obvious that he and Maria had fallen in love."

No romantic, Mitchell had never believed in love at first sight. "Can such instant attraction be called love? Surely real love takes time to develop."

Delia blushed profusely, though what there was in his remark to embarrass her, Mitchell could not even guess.

"All I know," she replied, "is that several months later William revealed to me that he and Maria had married in secret, and that she was with child. Maria's mother, like my own, had died in the influenza epidemic four years earlier, and since that time Maria had resided in her parents' town house with a paid companion. When Maria's condition became apparent, the affronted companion left her. That was when William brought her to me. It goes without saying that I was delighted to have her."

Mitchell did not think that such delight went without saying. In fact, in most instances the young woman would have been shunned by all who knew her. All save a true and devoted friend.

"Though I applaud your loyalty to your friend, I have to wonder why my cousin did not simply announce the marriage and take his wife home to Holcomb Park. He had to beard his father sooner or later. Why not then?"

"I asked that same question. All Maria would say was that William was employed in something very important—something that required him to remain in town for a time. She even spoke of it being a matter of life and death. Though until the night of his murder, I thought she—or perhaps William—had used that phrase merely for dramatic effect."

Delia swallowed, as though the sudden recalling of that night was bringing back disturbing memories. As if to lead the conversation down a less distressing path, she said, "My dear friend died, having proved too delicate to withstand the rigors of childbirth. William was heartbroken and tearfully entrusted Robbie to my care until such time as his business was finished and he could take the child himself."

"You did not mind, being saddled with another woman's child?"

She seemed surprised by the question. "Saddled? What a word to use when speaking of a child. Especially when I love Robbie with all my heart. I only hope that Sir Allistair will let me visit the lad from time to time. I will miss him so, once he is with his grandfather and I am returned to London."

"Returned to London!"

The very idea of her returning to the house where William was murdered made the muscles in Mitchell's stomach knot.

"My home is there," she said. "Of course, I dare not return as long as the murderer is at large and wishing me dead. After all, if he found me at Ems Regis, he can certainly find me in—"

"What do you mean, he found you in Ems Regis?" Before she could reply, Mitchell drew his own conclusions. "Georgie and his pal, they came to kill *you*. To silence you. I merely got in the way. You were their target all along." He drew in a ragged breath. "Why did you not tell me? Surely you did not think I would leave you to fend for yourself?"

She looked down at her feet, obviously not wanting to meet his eyes. "I could not tell you. At first, because I did not trust you, but later because I felt guilty for having gotten you involved. If anything had happened to you, I would never have been able to forgive myself for—"

Her voice broke, and Mitchell was obliged to restrain himself from putting his arms around her. What was it about Cordelia Barrington that had him angry with her one minute and wanting to take her in his arms the next, to shield her from pain?

She was undeniably beautiful, but he had known any number of beautiful women. She was also intelligent, and she was brave. He had seen bravery in all its forms, so he recognized it when he saw it. No matter how frightened Delia had become, no matter the danger to her, she had never given in, never forgotten that she was protecting an innocent child.

But there was more to it than that. There was something about her, some quality Mitchell could not put a name to. Whatever it was, it made him ready to do whatever was necessary to help her. "Do not fret on my account. I was not hurt, so no harm done."

She looked up at him then, and her eyes were filled with remorse. "But you might have been."

Fighting another urge to take her in his arms, he decided to let the subject drop, in order to pursue one that might prove more productive. "You never said which of those two men murdered my cousin. Was it Georgie or his accomplice?"

"Neither. Until they arrived at the cottage, I had never seen either of those men."

She paused, as if weighing her next words. "The man who murdered William was a different sort altogether. Smarter. Craftier. Crueler. Far more frightening. He killed without feeling. Without mercy. If that man had come to Ems Regis, I feel certain we would not have escaped."

They walked in silence for a time, Mitchell trying to recall everything he had overheard while lying on the parapet. Georgie and his accomplice had mentioned a peer. One they obviously feared. "This third man, the murderer, could he have been a peer?"

The question obviously surprised her, for her eyebrows shot up. "I do not believe so. He was small and stoop-shouldered, and his attire was more like that of a shopkeeper—dark, as if he did not wish to call attention to himself—with neither his coat nor his boots of any particular distinction. Furthermore, his speech was far from refined. However . . ."

"However?" Mitchell prompted.

"Seconds before William died, he said something about a peer. I was holding his hand, trying to encourage him not to give up until help arrived, but all he wanted to do was give me a message for someone—someone whose name I did not know and could not quite understand."

She looked up at Mitchell, as if to apologize for not being able to supply the name.

"Never mind," he said. "What was the message?"

"William had lost a lot of blood, you understand, and his breath was coming in shorter and shorter gasps, so I might have misunderstood."

"Just repeat what you heard."

She nodded. "First he told me to trust no one. Then he said to tell this person—his last name started with a *K* or a *C*—that it would happen at his lordship's ball."

"The ball! Yes."

"That has significance for you?"

Mitchell explained that Georgie had said something about a ball. "If I heard correctly, that ball was to be held in five days. That would be three days now."

"But whose ball is it? Where will it be held? And what is the 'it' that will happen there? What makes 'it' important enough to induce these men to do murder?"

Mitchell shrugged his shoulders. "So many questions, and none of them with answers. Or even the first clue."

The word had only just left his mouth when Delia caught his sleeve with both her hands. "The papers. The ones William gave me. Perhaps they contain the clue we need."

Mitchell had forgotten about the papers she had hidden at Sky Cottage. "I thought you said you had his wedding lines and proof that Robbie was his son."

"I did."

"As important as those papers are, they can hardly be expected to reveal anything about—" He paused, for Delia had turned a bright red. "There is more you have not told me."

She nodded. "I did not actually lie. I . . . I just failed to mention the packet. After all, William warned me to trust no one."

Mitchell bit back a swear word. "You have a packet belonging to my cousin?"

"Yes. At William's insistence, I took it from inside his coat. It consisted of letters wrapped in an oilskin and tied with a heavy string, so I knew it was important."

"Did you read the letters?"

She shook her head. "I never even looked inside. Unfortunately, William did not have time to tell me who should get the packet, so I planned to give it to Sir Allistair when I took Robbie to him, and let him do with it what he thought best."

Mitchell took her arm and turned her rather quickly in the direction of the garden entrance. "Come," he said, "we need to get those papers without delay. Before someone else finds—"

He got no further, for a pistol shot sounded from somewhere just behind them, and Delia cried out.

Training prompted Mitchell to drop to the ground with all speed; instinct made him throw himself against Delia and take her down with him, shielding her body with his own. Once they lay flat on the ground and were less of a target, he rolled off her and turned to look in the direction of the gun report. There was no one there. "Whoever it was," he said, "he is gone now."

Delia did not move. Not that Mitchell blamed her for being frightened. "You are safe," he assured her. "Come, give me your hand."

When she still did not move, he said, "You must let me help you up now, for we cannot remain here. We must be on our way to—

"Delia? Delia!"

She lay still as death, facedown in a bed of blue and purple pansies. The blue and purple were natural to the flowers, the red was not. The red was blood— Delia's blood—and an obscene amount of it was splattered all over the pansy petals.

Chapter Fourteen

During his nine years of military service, Mitchell had seen thousands of men wounded. He had seen hundreds of men die. But nothing in his past had prepared him for the fear that threatened to choke him as he gathered Delia in his arms and carried her back to the house. She lay limp as a rag doll, with blood covering the lower portion of her face and flowing down her neck at an alarming rate.

Running faster than he had ever run before, Mitchell shouted for someone—anyone to come to him.

"Sir!" said a stable lad who appeared from around the corner of the house.

"Ride to Chichester," Mitchell said. "Bring the apothecary at once. And if you value your job, do not return without him!"

"Aye, sir!" The lad touched his forelock in respect, then turned and ran toward the stables.

Meanwhile, the butler, upon hearing the commotion outside, swung open the entrance door, then stood there staring, as if turned to stone.

Lady Regina, who had come running from the morning room, a newspaper in her hands, stood just behind him in the vestibule. At sight of the unconscious girl in her son's arms, her ladyship kicked the ankle of the servant. "Do not stand there gaping like a veritable noddy," she said. "Go to the kitchen and fetch Mrs. Newly. And be quick about it! Tell her we need a basin of hot water and towels."

"Yes, my lady."

"In here," she instructed her son, "there is a fainting couch."

Mitchell followed his mother into the sun-filled morning room, and when he would have laid Delia on the petit point couch, with her head at the raised end, Lady Regina instructed him to turn her in the opposite direction. "Elevate her feet," she said, "for it will help to stanch the flow."

- It was not to be marveled at that Mitchell did as his mother bid him, for like most men, he felt all thumbs when faced with a wounded female. After depositing Delia on the couch, he moved aside, relieved to surrender her to Lady Regina's care.

"I heard only the one shot," he said, his voice noticeably unsteady, "but I did not have time to ascertain where the bullet entered."

"Bullet? What are you talking about, son? Miss Barrington is not shot."

"But she—"

"You may trust me on this, dear boy. Believe me, a woman cannot rear a son with your proclivity toward argumentation without being able to spot a nosebleed half a mile away."

His mother knelt beside the couch and began pinching Delia's nose with a small lace handkerchief, attempting to stop the bleeding. "What I do not understand," she said, "is how this could have happened." The words had no more than left her lips when she turned and looked up at her son. "Please tell me this is not to be laid at your door."

"Well, I— That is—" Quite certain the injury was completely his fault, Mitchell spoke rather sharply. "Surely you did not expect me to allow her to remain a standing target?"

*   *   *

"Madam," Delia said, an understandable degree of exasperation in her voice, "I begin to wonder if I shall survive the felons, only to be mortally wounded by your son and his rather peculiar notions of chivalry."

"The boy's an oaf," said his doting parent, "and you have every right to be angry with him."

"Angry does not begin to express my feelings. And if you knew the whole, ma'am, I am persuaded you would be in total sympathy with my feelings."

Lady Regina was more than agreeable to hearing the entire story, but when she expressed her willingness, the young lady blushed, her anger ebbing at a record pace.

"I . . . I shall not sully your ears, ma'am, with all the atrocities Mitchell Holcomb has committed upon my person in the name of saving me from harm. All things considered, I am fortunate that he pushed me into a flower bed, and not down some rocky ravine."

Mrs. Newly had come and gone with her water and towels, someone had been sent to stop the apothecary en route, and Mitchell was outside, searching the premises for the person who fired the shot that had, thankfully, not hit its intended target. Lady Regina and her son's bedraggled and blood-smeared guest were alone in the morning room.

It would have been an excellent opportunity for Miss Barrington to unburden herself about the relationship that existed between her and Mitchell, but to Lady Regina's regret, it appeared the young woman was not inclined to discuss the subject.

Curious, her ladyship studied Delia Barrington, who had insisted upon sitting up. A cold cloth had been applied to the back of her neck, and twists of cotton wool had been packed inside both her nostrils, just in case the ruptured vein should decide to spurt more blood. Aside from a small abrasion on her chin and one on her palm, where she had tried to break her fall, her injuries looked worse than they actually were.

What was it about this woman, Lady Regina wondered, that had her usually levelheaded son acting like a schoolboy experiencing his first *tendre*? She did not question the fact that he had feelings for the young woman, for she had never seen Mitchell so frightened as when he carried their unconscious guest into the house. His face had lost its healthy color, and his lips were drawn tightly against his teeth, as if to keep him from giving way to his fear.

Upon being convinced that Miss Barrington suffered from nothing more serious than a nosebleed, her son had emitted a heart-wrenching sigh. As Lady Regina watched, the color returned to his face, his fear turned to abject relief, then it became raw, red-eyed fury. Without a word, he had left the patient in her care, then marched through the corridor to the games room.

The last his mother saw of him, Mitchell was hurrying across the greensward toward the walled garden, a fowling piece in his hand and murder in the determined stiffness of his spine.

"Ah, yes," she said when a maid arrived with a tray containing a blue-and-white teapot and a plate of little bite-sized tarts, "just what we need." Once the servant had curtsied and left the room, Lady Regina poured a cup of the fragrant brew and passed it to her guest. "This should make you feel more the thing, Miss Barrington."

"Please, ma'am, call me Delia."

She watched Delia take a cautious sip of the steaming liquid, then a full drink.

"Umm."

"Nothing like a dish of tea. Do you not agree, my dear? Especially when one wishes to vilify gentlemen behind their backs. They can sometimes be such slowtops."

"Oh, no, ma'am! Not Mitchell."

In her haste to reply, her guest nearly spilled her

tea, though the entire pot could have been poured on the Gypsy clothes without significantly altering their grass- and blood-stained appearance. "Your son is anything but a slowtop, ma'am, for he is quite intelligent. And wonderfully forgiving. And so courageous. I vow, I do not know how I should have survived these past few days without him."

Ah, she defends him now, does she? "So, you are no longer angry with him?"

"Yes. No." She bit her lip in frustration. "It is just that he is so vexing, for he expects so much of me. He believes me to be this brave person, when I am not at all. And how he came to that conclusion, I cannot even guess."

"But you *are* brave, my dear. My son has told me about the murder, and about the two miscreants who followed him to Ems Regis. He informed me as well, that you have been protecting poor William's child. I was very much attached to my nephew, as was Mitchell, and I cannot tell you how grateful I am to you for keeping the little boy safe."

"I love him," her guest said simply, and from the dreamy look in Delia's eyes, Lady Regina wondered if she referred to the babe or to Mitchell.

"Are you quite certain you feel up to this?" Mitchell asked for perhaps the third time. "If not, we can wait until tomorrow."

"We cannot wait," Delia replied, "and you know it. You said the ball was in three days. Even if the packet is still where I hid it, which may not be the case if Georgie and his accomplice returned to search the cottage, we still do not know who to get in touch with about this entire mess."

"Please," Lady Regina said, "cease your arguing and get in the carriage. You both know what needs to be done. Now, do it."

Mitchell gave Delia his hand and helped her into

his mother's handsome black-and-gold berlin. Before he climbed in beside her, however, Lady Regina caught him by the sleeve to detain him. "I have taken the liberty of writing to your father and apprising him of everything that has occurred. I felt he would wish to know. I hope you do not mind."

"Father? No, I do not mind. I am curious, though. Is there some particular reason why you believe he might wish to know?"

She hesitated a moment. "I did not tell you this, Mitchell, principally because I did not think it had anything to do with this business in Ems Regis, but the day before your cousin's death, he came to the town house to see your father."

"William? To see Father? Do you know why?"

She shook her head. "I know no more than I have said. The matter must have been important, however, for the two of them remained in the book room, with the door locked, for fully two hours. And as soon as William left, Conrad called for his coach and went to speak to the prime minister."

"That is it!" Delia said, surprising mother and son by jumping down from the carriage. "Conrad. That was the name William mentioned, the one I did not quite understand."

Mitchell stared at her as though she were speaking in some foreign tongue. "You are certain he said Conrad?"

"I am sure of it. I thought he said two names, and something about the first name threw me off. Now I realize why. It was not a name at all. 'Tell *Uncle* Conrad,' he said, 'that it will happen at his lordship's ball.' "

Mitchell turned to his mother. "Have you posted the letter?"

"Not yet."

"Excellent. Be so good as to add another sheet, informing Father of William's dying message. Tell him as well, that once Delia and I have the packet in hand, we will bring it directly to him. I trust he will know what is to be done with it."

"Of course. I will do just as you say."

Mitchell signaled for the footman who stood just inside the door. "Her ladyship has a letter to be delivered to London. The moment it is ready, I wish you to take it to my father, who will be at his town house in Cavendish Square. Put it directly into his hands, and tell him that it is a matter of great urgency."

"Yes, sir. Right away, sir."

Without further ado, Delia and Mitchell bid Lady Regina good-bye, then climbed into the coach. As soon as the door was closed, the coachman cracked the whip and the team moved down the carriageway toward the gates.

Thanks to her ladyship's well-sprung berlin, their return trip to Ems Regis was far more comfortable than their departure two days ago. As well, the journey was accomplished in under two hours. It would have taken even less time had they not had to wait for half an hour just outside the village, due to high tide.

"Damnation," Mitchell muttered when the carriage came to a complete standstill behind a man riding a donkey and a farm wagon. "What cursed bad luck."

"It is the tides," Delia said. "Twice a day the Channel floods the area surrounding the village. This can be quite vexing when one is in a hurry, but since nothing can be done to hurry either time or the tides, the best course of action is to relax." As if taking her own advice, she laid her head against the black leather squabs and closed her eyes.

Mitchell was not fooled into thinking she meant to nap. "I came here often when I was a lad, so I know the rising waters can be treacherous."

She opened her eyes, all pretense of relaxing gone. "The tides are more than treacherous; they can be deadly. That is why the schedule of times is printed in the local newspaper. As well, there are warning signs posted at intervals along the beach."

"Yes, I am aware of—"

"One must be alert to the danger. Only days after I arrived at Nadja's, one of her guests disregarded the warnings and went for a long walk along the flood plain. He was not seen again until several days later when his body washed up off the Dorset coast."

An involuntary shudder ran through her, and Mitchell, recalling how frightened Delia was of the water, reached across and squeezed her hand. She allowed the familiarity for a few seconds; then, her eyes downcast, she slipped her hand from his.

Mitchell cursed beneath his breath. The last thing he wanted was for her to feel she had to be on guard in his presence. Hoping to recapture the easy camaraderie they had enjoyed earlier, he said, "As for the tides, you need have no concern, madam, for I have no plans to toss you into the rising water."

She gasped, but she no longer avoided eye contact.

"At least," he said calmly, "not today."

"Of all the—" She looked daggers at him, and Mitchell could not suppress a laugh.

"How nice," she said, her voice dripping sarcasm, "that I can offer you a bit of amusement to alleviate the boredom of waiting."

He tried to quench his laughter, but was only partially successful. "Take a bit of advice," he said, "and never try your luck at high stakes whist."

"Oh?" Curiosity, or her own naturally pleasant nature, overcame her momentary anger. "And why is that?"

"Because your thoughts show plainly on your face."

"And that is bad?"

"Very. With such a face, you are certain to be separated from your fortune before dawn."

"What a happy coincidence then, that I have no wish to play whist. High stakes or any other kind."

She tapped the sticking plaster that adorned her chin, covering the abrasion she received in the pansy bed. "With my luck, I should not need to wait for dawn. I would probably be a pauper by the second deal."

Having said that, she pursed her lips and whistled a few bars of "Without a Feather to Fly With."

Mitchell laughed aloud. "Where the devil did a gently reared young lady learn so many low tunes?"

"Oh," she said, batting her eyes as if that would convince him of her innocence, "is that song not respectable?"

"Minx. You know it is not."

The sound of her laughter was delightful.

In the past few days, there had been few light-hearted moments, and Mitchell found himself wishing he could make this moment last. Delia was smiling, and even with the sticking plaster on her chin, she was beautiful . . . so beautiful that just looking at her made his pulses race.

The Gypsy skirt and bodice she had worn during their original flight had seen far too much action and had finally been relegated to the rag pile. Now she wore a pretty pomona green traveling dress given to her by his mother. The coffee-colored spencer and matching jockey bonnet might have been made for her, for they were a perfect complement to her eyes.

Those bright eyes smiled up at him now, and Mitchell was sorely tempted to take her soft face between his hands and kiss her eyelids. After that, it would be so easy to rain kisses down that pert little nose, finally coming to a stop at her luscious lips. At the thought of claiming her mouth and searching its sweetness with his tongue, he felt his neckcloth tighten dangerously around his Adam's apple, obliging him to run his finger inside the starched linen to loosen the knot.

Damnation! How was a man supposed to keep his distance when the woman mere inches away was so lovely and so completely oblivious to the effect of that loveliness? And apparently oblivious to how badly he wanted to take her in his arms and make love to her.

"How the deuce has a woman with your looks remained unwed?" He had not meant to voice his thoughts, and he was as surprised as she was by the question. "Er, what I mean is, have you something against the married state?"

Mitchell had wanted to preserve the lighthearted moment, and with that one question, he had shattered it completely. Her eyes no longer smiled; instead, they become sober, pensive.

"I have nothing against marriage," she said. "In fact, I was once betrothed."

Betrothed! Mitchell could not believe the primitive anger that one word instilled in him.

Delia had once had a fiancé! Just the thought of another man having the right to hold that lovely body in his arms, to kiss those lips, to whisper words of love to her, made Mitchell want to drive his sword through the unknown knave's heart.

"Who?" he asked, his voice sounding sharper than he had intended. "Where is he now?"

"Dead," she replied quietly. "Killed at Trafalgar."

She turned her face away, as though unwilling to share the painful memory, and Mitchell felt as if it was his own heart that had been run through. Her fiancé was dead. A naval hero more than likely, and from her reaction, chances were she loved him still.

No wonder she had been cool to Mitchell this morning in the garden. She loved another. And how, he wondered, was a mere mortal to compete with a dead hero?

Chapter Fifteen

Sky Cottage looked much as it had two days ago when they last saw it, except that the front door no longer stood open. Recalling how Georgie had seemed to come from nowhere, his cudgel raised, Delia prayed that he was not waiting to ambush them the moment they entered the cottage.

Mitchell and the coachman were both armed with pistols, but to Delia's relief, the weapons were not needed. The cottage was empty. The place had been ransacked, with furniture overturned and the contents of the cupboard strewn across the floor, but if Georgie and the other fellow were looking for the packet, they did not find it.

Mitchell sent the coachman to the barn to see to the horses and curricle he had been obliged to leave there, then he and Delia climbed the stairs to the bedchamber she and Robbie had shared. The two men had been there as well. The bed was overturned, the drawers of the chest had been emptied onto the floor, and the mattress ticking had been slashed with a knife and the feather stuffing pulled out. Feathers covered every surface, and with even the slightest breeze they flew into the air only to resettle in some new place.

Delia had brought a knife up from the kitchen, and now she knelt on the floor and used the tip of the blade to pry up a loose floorboard. Upon spying the oilskin-wrapped packet, along with a few other papers, all tied together with a hair ribbon, she closed her eyes, as if offering up a silent word of thanksgiving.

"Here," she said, quickly passing the lot to Mitchell. He had joined her on the floor, one long leg stretch out in front of him, the other bent so that his arm rested on his raised knee. "You open them."

He had no trouble understanding her reticence, for the oilskin bore several rusty spots that must surely be blood—William's blood.

Telling himself not to think about that, Mitchell untied the incongruous pink hair ribbon and set aside the loose papers. He would read those later. For now, there were more important things to discover.

After folding back the oilskin flaps, he lifted out half a dozen letters and a much-handled sheet of foolscap. He began with the foolscap, which bore a rough sketch of someone's town house and back garden. On the sketch, large check marks had been placed at each of the ground-floor doors and windows, and there were lines to indicate the path from the mews to the garden entrance.

Delia had moved around behind him, so that she could look over his shoulder. "What do you make of it?" she asked.

"At a guess, I would say it is the home of the mysterious peer, and the site of the coming ball." He pointed to two adjoining parlors on the second floor. "With the furniture removed and the pocket doors open, this area would serve for dancing."

"And," Delia added, "for the peer's nefarious plans, whatever they may be."

As if spurred by her remark, Mitchell took three of the letters and gave the other three to her. "Read," he said. It was not a request, but an order, and though Delia was inclined to remind him that she was not one of his subalterns, she held her tongue, for she realized that he felt a sense of urgency.

Surrendering to the inevitable, she opened the first sheet, which had once been secured by a plain, cheap wafer. There was no salutation and no signature, merely the body of the letter, which had to do with supplies and quartermasters and some man whose name Delia did not recognize.

The next letter was every bit as uninformative, for it dealt with the purchase of a pair of dueling pistols reputed to have belonged to the grandfather of Lord Horatio Nelson, the naval hero.

"Anything?" Mitchell asked.

Delia shook her head. "Not unless you are interested in the sale of a set of dueling pistols."

Mitchell looked as puzzled as she felt. "Dueling pistols? What have they to say to anything sinister?"

"I cannot say. Now that dueling is against the law, is there any questions of the legalities of owning such weapons?"

"Not that I have heard."

"Nor I. But it may be a moot point, for this letter sounds as if it was written not by a hopeful user of the weapons, but a collector."

Mitchell had gone back to the sheet he was reading, but he looked up long enough to ask her about the other letter she had read. "Have either of yours got signatures?"

"No, nor salutations, so I cannot see how we are ever to discover the identity of the nefarious peer."

"And the body of the letter?" he asked.

"I fear it is no more informative than the one about the pistols. Unless, of course, one is interested in the doings of quartermasters."

To Delia's surprise, Mitchell all but snatched the paper from her hands, then began to read it aloud. "Yes," he said once he had finished, "believe it or not, this is a clue of sorts. Or it may well be to my father, who has been interested of late in a group of well-connected men who have been profiteering from questionable practices in the buying and selling of war supplies.''

Delia *tsk-tsked,* sorry to be reminded that there existed the sort of men who thought of war in terms of profits rather than in terms of human sacrifice and loss. If such men were involved in William's murder, then the "it" that was to happen at the ball could only be something reprehensible.

Hoping to find a more productive clue, she unfolded the third letter, which was noticeably longer than the first two. The handwriting was the same, and as before, no names were mentioned.

The date is fixed for the twenty-ninth of May. Though the "object" will arrive late, as is his usual practice, most of the guests will begin arriving around nine o'clock. For that reason, you must have your men in place no later than eight o'clock.

There will be time for only one shot, so I am trusting that the men are, as you promised, expert marksmen.

As planned, you and I will have been admiring my latest set of dueling pistols, which I will leave on the desk in my library. As the marksmen run from the ballroom, you will shoot the one on the left, I will shoot the one on the right. By so doing, we will rid ourselves of the assassins, and we will probably gain a medal as heroes.

After that, it will not matter who wins the election, we will be able to continue as before.

Delia gasped and let the letter fall from her hands. "Assassins," she said, the word all but sticking in her throat.

"What?" Mitchell asked.

"The 'it,' the thing that will take place at the ball. It is an assassination!"

She began to shake so badly that Mitchell put down the sheet he was reading and took both her hands. "Does the letter give the name of the person who is to be murdered?"

"N . . . no. Not a name. Only that the person usually comes late to such functions."

Mitchell looked deep into her eyes, as if willing her to think, though she suspected he could give her a name if he wished to. "Who comes late?" he asked, "on a regular basis."

Delia could not think. "I have been away from the social scene for some time, but there are always those people who consider it fashionable to be the last to arrive at any party. I have never been one of their number, but—"

"Think," he said, the word an order. "If you were giving a ball, who would be the one person you would forgive for being late?"

"I do not know. I suppose it would have to be someone whose personality or superior social standing were such that by merely attending my party he or she would guarantee that it was a success. A person of elevated rank would do the trick."

"And?" Mitchell prompted, "who might that person be?"

She shook her head. "I cannot say. There are several such persons. One of the royal dukes, perhaps. Maybe even Prinny himself, for he enjoys attending— No!"

"Yes," Mitchell said. "The Regent himself. It is the only thing that makes sense."

"Sense! It is the most nonsensical thing I ever heard. Who would wish to assassinate the Prince Regent? And why? Aside from stepping into the gap left by his poor father's diminished health, Prinny has done nothing to instill such hatred in his subjects. True, he has overspent egregiously, but—"

"Concentrate on the fact of his regency. Then re-read your first letter."

"But you said that was about profiteering? What has the Prince Regent to do with profiteering?"

"Nothing, as yet."

Delia sighed in exasperation. "As yet? What does that mean?"

"Please," he said, "bear with me, for I am thinking aloud, and I need you to keep me from going overboard in my surmises." He looked at her then and smiled. "We make such a good team."

When he smiled at her that way, with those amazing gray eyes looking directly into hers, all but pleading with her to do as he asked, Delia could do nothing but capitulate. "Continue," she said.

"As you may already know, Prinny is an avowed Whig."

"Everyone knows that. Though, personally, I cannot believe the prince is all that political. He is very much a lover of pleasure, and such men are seldom ardent about anything else."

"You may be right."

"I hear a 'however' just waiting."

"However," he said, then winked at her, "Prinny's true feelings and lifestyle notwithstanding, now that he has been made Regent he has it in his power to replace the present Tory leadership with Whigs."

"What nonsense! My stepfather was not a fan of the present prime minister, but I have heard him say more than once that Spencer Perceval was as canny a man as ever served his country. Surely Perceval will know how to handle the Prince Regent.

"Besides," she continued, "Prinny may be a portly, middle-aged fellow with an indolent nature, but he is not stupid. He has ever-mounting debts that want paying, and I cannot believe he would wreck his chances at solvency by calling for a dissolution of the government."

"I tend to agree with you."

"Do I hear another 'however'?"

"Yes. The problem is that the men involved in this assassination plot will want to make *certain* there is no dissolution. If the government should fall, these men have much to lose. If the Whigs should come to power, there would be the inevitable domino effect of reappointments, and the present profiteers would lose their connections to the supply chains. And along with forfeiting their connections, they could lose millions of pounds in future illegal revenues."

Delia whistled. "So much money. No wonder they are willing to do murder. But who are these men who would plot to kill the heir to the throne?"

"That piece of information we have yet to learn. I suspect my cousin knew, however, and that knowledge is what got him killed. William was murdered to keep him quiet. And," Mitchell added, motioning toward the sheets of paper that lay scattered among the mattress feathers, "to regain the very incriminating evidence contained in the packet."

Delia's mouth was so dry she could barely swallow. "And that is why they sent Georgie after me. Not because I saw the actual murderer—surely such malefactors know how to simply disappear. No, those men want me because I took the packet."

"Exactly. And you will continue to be in danger until we can turn these papers over to the proper authorities."

"Your father?" she asked.

"For want of a better person, yes. My father will know who will have authority to act upon this information, and act swiftly."

"Then let us waste no more time."

Delia began gathering up the letters and the oilskin, her aversion to touching the bloodstained items giving way to necessity. "If we go now," she said, "we can be in London before nightfall."

For the next five hours, Mitchell and Delia spoke very little. While the berlin covered the sixty-plus miles to London, with the scenery changing from stark, dramatic seacoast, to lush green downs, then to pretty, prosperous farm lands, the occupants of the coach were lost in private thoughts. They paid little attention to the changing scenery, for they were both intent upon assimilating all they had learned of the assassination plot.

The coachman stopped only when necessary, and then only long enough to allow the inn's ostlers to change the horses. At some point during the journey, Delia fell asleep, lulled by the sway of the carriage and reassured by the notion that Mitchell watched over her, his pistol on the seat beside him, at the ready should anyone try to intercept their coach.

As for Mitchell, he felt his responsibility much too strongly to allow him to close his eyes. Besides, while Delia slept, he could look at her as often and as long as he wished, enjoying the way her long, dark lashes touched her creamy skin, and the tempting way her lips parted with each soft breath.

While he watched over Delia, he read and reread the papers from the packet, searching for any missed clues. When the coachman finally reined in the horses before his parents' elegant town house in Cavendish Square, Mitchell had a fair notion of who might be the host of the coming ball. He would keep his thoughts to himself, however, until he had spoken to his father.

"My boy," Conrad Holcomb said the moment his son passed through the entrance door, "I received your mother's letter two hours ago, and since that time, I have done nothing but haunt the front windows, waiting for your arrival."

Father and son shook hands, then Mitchell spared a moment to introduce Delia.

Conrad Holcomb bowed over Delia's hand. "Miss Barrington."

Delia curtsied to the distinguished, gray-haired gentleman, who was an older version of Mitchell, though more serene and less physically imposing than his son. "It is a pleasure to meet you, sir."

"The pleasure is all mine, my dear, though I wish we could have met under more felicitous circumstances. And," he added, a teasing smile on his lips, "I hope one day to be allowed a glimpse of you in the bewitching Gypsy attire my wife mentioned in her letter."

Ignoring the heat that rushed to her cheeks, Delia readily accepted her host's offer of a tray of tea and sandwiches.

After he ordered the tray prepared and brought to the book room, Conrad Holcomb ushered the new arrivals into that private and very masculine sanctuary, where they might speak without being overheard. "Now," he said, "what have you to show me?"

By the time the refreshments arrived, he had read each of the letters, scanned the foolscap drawing, and listened to what Delia had to relate about the murder of William Holcomb, as well as his final message about "it" happening at his lordship's ball.

For the most part, Mitchell let Delia do the talking, adding his mite only when she left out some particular fact. Still, he was surprised when she asked his father if he could not just ascertain the name of the person hosting a ball in three days' time, and have the authorities arrest him.

"I wish it were that easy, Miss Barrington. Unfortunately, there are three balls being given on Friday, and two of them are being hosted by peers. Would you have them both arrested?"

"Why, no. I just thought—"

"Furthermore, it is not all that easy to arrest a member of the nobility. One must be very careful about making accusations willy-nilly, especially, when there are such stiff penalties for slander."

While his father explained the laws protecting citizens from defamation and false accusation, Mitchell let his mind wander. The book-lined room, with its oversize leather chairs and its heavy drapery, was having a disquieting effect upon him. He could not rid his mind of the idea that he sat in the same room where his father had last met with William Holcomb, possibly occupying the same brown wing chair his cousin had occupied at that time.

He could almost feel his cousin's presence.

Mitchell was much larger than William. Had the wing chair groaned when his cousin settled comfortably in it? Had the leather squeaked each time he moved, as it did now? Had he stretched his legs out as Mitchell was doing, and had his boot heels left half-moon imprints in the claret-colored carpet?

Sadness settled on Mitchell as he remembered the happy boy who had followed him about as a lad. That smiling lad was gone forever. He may actually have been gone for years, without Mitchell realizing it. Now, considering all he had learned in the past few days, Mitchell was obliged to alter his concept of his cousin's adult life.

To that end, he recalled something Sir Allistair's man of business had said to him. Lester Venton had suggested the likelihood of William's having formed interests and loyalties of which Mitchell was totally unaware. At the time he had thought it impossible, but now everything pointed to its being true. His cousin had been some sort of spy, and because of the occupation he had chosen, he had forfeited his own life and risked the life of an innocent young woman.

At the thought of all Delia had endured, through no fault of her own, Mitchell's sadness became overlaid with anger, and he swore beneath his breath. "For whom was William working?"

His father hesitated, and for a moment Mitchell thought he meant not to answer. "For the Home Department," he said at last.

"But why? It is not as if there are not men enough

to do the job of domestic spying. Men toughened by life and more able to deal with the dangers involved. Men who need employment. William was Sir Allistair's heir, and he had a very generous allowance. He might have done anything he chose."

"As you might have," his father said quietly. "Yet you chose to become a soldier. A very dangerous way of life, the military."

His father gave him time to assimilate the implied comparison before he continued.

"As you may remember, William was always an adventurous lad, much too full of energy and drive to remain idle. Yet he had no taste for the clergy, and he possessed insufficient patience and tact for the diplomatic life. When your uncle would not hear of his only child following your example and entering the military, William offered his services to the Home Department."

"And did you know about this, sir?"

"Not until several years after the fact. Not until your cousin came to me to tell me about the plot to assassinate His Royal Highness. William trusted me, both as a member of Parliament and as a member of his family. He wanted me to know what was afoot, in case something happened to him."

A knock sounded at the library door. It was the butler informing his employer that the *vis-à-vis* was out front.

"Tell John coachman I will be there momentarily."

Surprised that his father was going out, Mitchell asked where he was bound.

"To Whitehall, my boy, to lay this entire plot before the secretary. With the letters from the packet to support the story, I am certain the secretary will do all that is necessary to insure the Prince Regent's safety."

"And bring to justice the person who murdered my cousin?"

"That, too," replied his father.

He rose to take his departure, but hesitated long enough to instruct his butler to have one of the housemaids take Miss Barrington abovestairs and attend her. "If the blue bedchamber is prepared, it should do nicely, I think."

"No, no," she said. "I thank you for your kind offer of hospitality, sir, but I am persuaded it is time I returned to Grosvenor Square, to my own home."

"No!" Mitchell said.

"I must," she said.

Conrad Holcomb looked from his son to the young lady, then lifted her hand to his lips. "I would be honored to have you as my guest, Miss Barrington, but it shall be as you wish."

"She is staying," his son said, his tone emphatic.

"No, sir. I am not," she replied, her tone equally assertive.

A wise man knew the value of retreat, and Conrad Holcomb was nothing if not wise. "I will leave you two to work out the details. In any event, my dear Miss Barrington, we will meet again, I am quite certain of it.

"My boy," he said, laying his hand on his son's shoulder.

"Father," Mitchell replied through clenched teeth.

In political circles, Conrad Holcomb was known as a very downy fellow; it was a sobriquet he had earned many times over. Still, it did not require a heightened intellect to realize that something was afoot here—something other than an assassination plot.

His son and Miss Delia Barrington were staring daggers at one another, and from the determined set of their respective chins, there was soon to be waged in his book room a battle royal.

"Hmm," he muttered as he made his way to his waiting coach. "How very interesting."

Chapter Sixteen

The berlin had reached Delia's town house on Grosvenor Street, and the two inhabitants were still arguing about her insistence upon returning to her home. "Please," Delia said, "I am here, and it is what I want. Can we not say our farewells without rancor?"

"Farewells? Is this your opinion of me? That I would politely shake your hand, then drive away, not caring who or what might be waiting for you behind that door?"

From the belligerent tone of Mitchell's voice, Delia decided there was no good way to answer his question. When she said nothing, his belligerence gave way to frustration. "Madam, the last time I came to this house, I walked right in, for there was not even one servant on the premises to stop me. For that reason, if for none other, you cannot enter that house alone."

"Tomorrow I will notify the servants that I have returned, and they will—"

"Tomorrow! What of tonight? If you think I will allow you to remain here without so much as an abigail in attendance, then you do not possess even half the intelligence I give you credit for. In short, your damned attic is to let!"

Far from being insulted, Delia was much inclined to fall on his neck and kiss him for insisting upon accompanying her. The very last thing she truly wished to do was walk into that house knowing she would be all alone.

Nor, for that matter, did she wish to say good-bye to Mitchell. Conrad Holcomb might believe they would all meet again, but Delia was not so certain. Mitchell had come into her life unexpectedly, and because he had no idea of the chaos he had created inside her heart, she was certain he would go out of her life without a backward glance. Not that she faulted him for it; after all, he had no idea that she loved him to the very depth of her soul.

There! She admitted it. She loved him. With all her heart. Without reservation, and for eternity.

Blissfully unaware of the thoughts going through her mind, Mitchell retrieved the pistol from where it still lay on the seat and tucked the weapon into the waistband of his breeches. Reluctantly, he stepped out of the coach, then turned and helped her to alight. Once they were on the pavement, he told the coachman to return to Cavendish Square. "I feel the need for some air, so once I have seen Miss Barrington safely inside, I will walk home."

"Aye, sir."

After tipping his hat respectfully, the coachman gave the horses the signal to be on their way. The rattle of the carriage wheels was already fading into the distance by the time Delia climbed the three steps to the small landing, opened the heavy oak door, and entered the dim and eerily silent vestibule. Within moments, she found the phosphorous box and lit the brace of candles that always reposed on the console table.

The house felt cold, almost clammy, and after two months of sitting empty, it smelled more than a little musty. A film of dust had settled on the black-and-white marble tiles that covered the floor of the vestibule and continued down the short corridor leading to the rear of the house.

"See," she said, trying to sound cheerful in the face of so much abject dreariness, "no one has been here. If they had, they would have left footprints in the dust."

Obviously, Mitchell was in no mood to be amused, for he took her by the arm and led her up the green-carpeted stairs, the candelabra held high so they could see where they put their feet. When they reached the landing, he lit the candles in one of the brass wall sconces, then asked which was her bedchamber.

"There," she said, pointing to the right, to one of the four rooms on that floor. "Why?"

He let go of her arm and stepped in front of her. "Stay here," he said, "while I have a look inside."

The words were an order rather than a request, but Delia did not even think about objecting. She was far too happy not to be here alone. She had not once imagined that the house would feel so lonely, so un-cared for, and this homecoming was proving far more difficult than she had imagined.

Mitchell pushed open the bedchamber door and went inside. After a minute he returned. "The room is empty, and I have lit the candles for you."

"Er, thank you. I—"

"Do not thank me, just promise me you will do as I say."

At her nod of agreement, he continued. "There is a key in the lock. Go inside and turn it. Allow me at least twenty minutes to search the house, beginning with the attic rooms."

"And if you have not returned by the allotted time? What then?"

He considered the question for a moment. "At that time, feel free to open your window, hang your head out, and scream for all you are worth."

When she could not hide her smile, he gave her a look that probably turned young soldiers to stone. "And under no circumstances, madam, are you to unlock that door until I say you may. Is that clearly understood?"

Delia lifted her hand to her forehead in a military salute. "Understood, Major. Thank you, Major. Any further orders, Major?"

"Yes," he said, "try not to be such a hoyden."

Mitchell heard her laughter even after the bedchamber door was closed and the key turned in the lock.

As he took the stairs to the attic rooms two at a time, he recalled a boast he had made to Sir Allistair's attorney just one week ago. "I have dealt with threats and attempted intimidation from hardened soldiers," he had said. "Believe me, bringing a cheeky female to heel should prove to be a simple matter."

Ha! There was a boast worthy of a fool!

One cheeky female in particular had proven unconscionably difficult to bring to heel. Especially when the only place Mitchell really wanted to bring her was into his arms.

Reminding himself that he had a job to do, he searched every corner of the attic, then walked through each of the lower rooms, holding the candelabra aloft so that no niche went unexamined. After shooting home the bolt on the front door, he checked the ground floor rooms and inspected the locks at the windows. He ended his search in the kitchen, where he made certain the bolt on the service door was securely fastened. When he was convinced that all was secure, he returned to Delia's bedchamber and knocked at her door.

"It is I," he said.

She remained on the other side of the locked door, but when he heard her smother a laugh, Mitchell imagined he could see her face, her eyes alight with amusement.

"I forget," she said, "did we agree upon a password?"

"Damnation, Delia. This is serious business."

"Of course, it is. But anyone could say, 'It is I' in that deep, military-sounding voice. How do I know it is *truly* you. What if you are not who you say you are, but are, in fact, some malefactor bent on evil deeds? In such an instance, I would do well to follow instructions and hang out my window, screaming until some good Samaritan came to my rescue."

Cheeky wench!

"Madam, you may do whatever suits you, but I suggest you get some rest. As for me, I found a decanter of brandy, and I have taken it to a pleasant little room that overlooks the rear garden. By now, the fire should be going nicely in there, and I mean to make use of one of those inviting, overstuffed chairs and enjoy a drink beside the hearth. I shall remain in that room until morning, so you may sleep without fear."

"You . . . you are staying? But you told the coachman—"

"That was for the protection of your reputation. Surely you did not think I would leave you here alone."

"I did not know."

All cheekiness was gone from her voice, and the absence left her sounding quite young and vulnerable. "Thank you, Mitchell."

When she said nothing more, he wished her pleasant dreams, then took the stairs down to the little room where the French windows allowed a moonlit view of the garden. It was a snug space, filled to capacity by a fruitwood lady's desk and two chintz-covered wing chairs. The fire had taken the chill out of the air, and in the cozy half-light Mitchell felt quite at home.

Hoping to make himself even more comfortable, he laid the pistol on the side table, struggled to remove his top boots, then rid himself of his coat, his waistcoat, and his neckcloth. After pouring himself a snifter of brandy, he settled into one of the high-backed chairs and stretched his stockinged feet toward the slate hearth.

Never much of a man for spirits, he had one drink, then part of another before his eyelids began to feel heavy. Soon, he felt himself slipping into oblivion. He slept, but it might have been for five minutes or five hours. All he knew was that some sound roused him and suddenly he was wide awake.

Immediately, he reached for the pistol he had left on the table beside the decanter. When he eased back the hammer, the unmistakable sound echoed inside the small room.

"Do not shoot," Delia said. "It is only me."

She stood just inside the doorway, and when Mitchell eased the hammer back into place and returned the pistol to the table, she crossed the room to the fire, which had burned itself down to nothing more than glowing embers. "I did not mean to wake you," she said. "I . . . I was cold. I just wanted to sit by the fire."

She wore a plain lawn wrapper over her nightrail, but she had thrown a woolen shawl over her shoulders. Even with the warm shawl, her hands trembled noticeably.

Mitchell said nothing, merely found the coal bucket, placed several shovelfuls of coal on the embers, then used the poker to prod the fire back to life.

When he took Delia's hands, her fingers were icy cold. "Come," he said, tugging gently, yet giving her ample opportunity to tell him nay, if that was her wish. "You may sit with me until the fire is going properly."

She offered no resistance, so he pulled her down onto his lap and wrapped his arms around her. She sighed, then fitted her soft body against his so naturally that they might have been sitting thus for years. When she snuggled her head on his shoulder and her warm breath teased his bare neck, it was the most natural thing in the world for him to nuzzle his jaw against the top of her head.

Her hair hung in a loose braid down her back, and the silken tresses smelled like heaven. She felt like heaven in his arms, all vulnerable and sleepy, and without even trying she affected him as no other woman ever had. It felt so good to hold this woman in his arms. This woman . . . his Delia.

Though he knew it was insanity to remain in such a potentially volatile position, he willed the fire not to take hold, not to warm the room. He wanted to hold her close—to warm her—for just a little while longer. He wanted to feel her softness, to absorb the sweetness of her.

He did not feel her move her head, and yet her soft lips somehow found their way to his exposed throat. At the first, light contact, he jerked his head back. Had she meant to touch him, or was it an accident? Accident or intent, his pulses quickened and fire ignited in every part of his body.

As if to convince him that the contact had been intentional, she lifted her face and pressed a light kiss on the underside of his chin. Then another. And another.

"Delia," he whispered, his voice so husky he barely recognized it as his own, "this is insanity. Do you know what you are doing?"

"No," she said, her voice sounding every bit as unsteady as his own. "But I am a very quick learner. That is, if you will cooperate just the least little bit."

Cooperate! Heaven help him, he had never wanted anything so badly in his entire life. Every muscle, every nerve in his body ached to cooperate. It required all his willpower just to stop himself from laying her down on the carpet in front of the hearth and showing her just how cooperative a fellow he could be.

"Kiss me," she whispered. "Just this once."

Not impervious to her soft pleading, he said, "Just this once," then he put his hand beneath her chin and turned her face up to his. "How can I resist you, when you are so beautiful?"

"Am I?"

"Oh, yes," he said, then he bent his head and claimed her mouth. He kissed her again and again, and each kiss was sweeter than the one before it.

At some point she had wound her arms around his neck, and now, with her soft breasts pressed against his chest, he could feel her heart beating wildly, like a frightened deer. Or was that his heart? No, he had no heart; if he had, he would send her away before the kisses got out of hand. Before he compromised her entirely.

When she moaned softly, then shyly touched the tip of her tongue to his lips, Mitchell knew it was already too late to send her away. He wanted her, and he was quite certain he would go mad if he could not have her.

"My beautiful, beautiful girl," he murmured. He had begun to rain kisses down the side of her slender neck, all but lost in the feel and taste of her, when his concentration was shattered by the sound of breaking glass.

The French windows!

Quickly scooping Delia into his arms, he slid to the floor. "Shh," he warned. With his mouth close to her ear, he whispered for her to lie very still. "The high back of the chair hid us from view, and I do not think they realize we are here."

Slowly, cautiously, Mitchell reached up to the table and found the pistol. With the weapon in hand, he crawled on his stomach, moving as far away as possible from Delia and the firelight. Using the writing desk for cover, he raised his head enough to see the French windows.

On the other side of the glass, a man's shape was silhouetted in the moonlight. Thank heaven, it was just the one man.

While Mitchell watched, the intruder reached his right arm through the broken pane and began fumbling with the lock. Mitchell, quite certain he did not want to allow the fellow inside the room, cocked the pistol and aimed it just above and to the right of the bent arm. "Halt!" he ordered.

"Gor blimey!" the man muttered, obviously surprised that he was not alone.

"Be warned!" Mitchell said, his voice booming so there was no mistaking his words. "I have a pistol aimed at your heart, and if you are not gone in three seconds, I will shoot you down like the mad dog you are."

"Bloody 'ell!"

The intruder did not need the full three seconds, for on the instant he pulled his arm back through the broken glass, turned, and fled toward the rear of the garden.

Mitchell heard the muffled footfalls on the lawn, but by the time he reached the French windows, the man had disappeared behind the hedge that separated the garden from the alleyway to the mews. "He is gone," he said. "You can get up now."

Delia sat up, but she did not attempt to stand. Instead, she hugged her bent knees to her chest and rested her forehead on her right knee. All was silent save for the crackling of the fire, and in the quiet, Mitchell heard the unmistakable sound of weeping.

In the past, women's tears had made him want to run for the nearest door. But not this time. Delia had been so brave for so long, and if anyone deserved a good cry, it was her. All Mitchell wanted to do was hold her close and comfort her. To be there if she needed him.

"Please," he said, taking her by the arms and helping her to stand, "do not cry. I promise you, you are safe."

It was a full minute before she finally spoke, and when she did her voice was watery from the tears she tried to hold back. "I do not believe I will ever feel safe again," she said, "for this nightmare appears destined never to end."

"It will end," Mitchell said, "you have my word on it. Even if I must personally put a bullet through Lord Leeland's heart."

Chapter Seventeen

"*L*ord Leeland? Mitchell, are you insane? The man is nothing more than a popinjay. An affected coxcomb who—"

"Who has tried more than once to have you killed."

She shook her head. "You cannot know that. True, he is hosting a ball on Friday, but your father said there were two peers hosting balls on that evening. The other peer could be the culprit."

"He could be, but I doubt it."

Delia just could not make the image she held of the lisping Lord Leeland conform to that of a cold-blooded murderer. "But I have known his lordship for years. My parents knew him. He . . . he just cannot be the person who had William murdered."

They spent the next two hours discussing the likelihood of Lord Leeland's being the man behind the assassination plot, with neither of them changing their opinion on the matter. In time, they noticed that the sun had risen, and Mitchell said it was time for him to leave.

While Delia went abovestairs and changed into a carriage dress of a most fetching primrose, topped by a spencer of bronze faille, and completed by a matching Dutch bonnet whose upturned front revealed several wispy curls she had combed over her forehead,

Mitchell put himself back together. After pulling on his boots, he did his best arranging a sadly rumpled cravat, then donned his waistcoat and coat.

By the time Delia returned, he had reclaimed his beaver hat and was waiting for her beside the French windows. "You are certain you are not nervous about remaining here until I return?"

"Quite," she replied. "Just *you* be certain you do not get lost."

He gave her an affronted look. "Madam, I *never* get lost. Once or twice I may have found myself on an unscheduled route, but I was never lost."

"Ah, yes. Unscheduled. What would life be without euphemisms?"

"What indeed?" he asked.

He was still chuckling when he let himself out the French windows and strolled purposefully across the dew-kissed garden toward the alleyway that led to the mews. Once he was out of sight, Delia closed and locked the French windows, then went around to the entrance door, where she waited patiently.

Within a matter of minutes, a hackney carriage stopped before the town house on Grosvenor Street, and a tall, muscular gentleman climbed out. Instructing the jarvey to wait, he climbed the three steps to the door, then sounded the knocker. Moments later, the door was opened by a lady in a primrose carriage dress.

"Miss Barrington," the gentleman said, loud enough for any interested parties to hear, "you are very prompt. An admirable trait in one of your sex."

The lady in primrose curtsied. "Good morning, Major Holcomb, you are prompt as well. An *unexpected* trait in a member of your sex."

The gentleman chuckled, then he took the lady's arm and assisted her down the steps to the pavement and into the waiting hackney. "Whew," he said, once they were safely inside the carriage, "I think we pulled it off. I cannot believe your neighbors are any the wiser that I stayed the night in your house."

"So, the proprieties are observed, if not met."

"At least, your good name remains unblemished."

"Yes," she said. "Let us hope I live long enough to enjoy the reputation we have so assiduously guarded."

The humor was gone instantly from his face. "That is why we are stopping by Bow Street. For the next two days, I want a couple of their most intimidating Runners watching you at all times."

Delia made no objections to the arrangement, but under no circumstances would she allow Mitchell to defray the costs. For that reason, before they stopped at Bow Street, she asked if they might visit her bank at twenty-four Lombard Street.

While at the bank, she accomplished two things that made her feel much more like her old self. First, she obtained enough money to meet her present personal and domestic needs, and second, she asked her banker, Mr. Whitmore, if one of his assistants would be so good as to take messages to her housekeeper and her butler, informing those two members of her staff that their employer had returned to town and hoped to see them in Grosvenor Square as soon as may be.

"So," Mitchell said, once they were again in the hackney, "you knew all along where the servants had gone. They did not desert you."

"Of course they did not. Why, they have been with the family for years. They left the house because I told them to do so. After all, I could not flee the killer and leave them there to face danger that was none of their doing."

The statement being unarguable, they quit the bank and continued to Bow Street, where they told only as much of the story as was necessary to insure Delia's protection. By the time they left that establishment, two large and exceedingly pugnacious-looking men were already on the job.

When Mitchell and Delia stopped at Filburt's, off St. James's, to break their fast with tea and freshly baked seedcakes, the two "red breasts" stood just outside the gold-and-white door, alternating between frightening the customers on the other side of the tea shop's plate-glass window and scowling at those pedestrians who were so unfortunate as to walk past the establishment. Later, when Delia entered a draper's shop to order material for two dozen nappies for young Robbie, the burly duo stood among the satin ribbons and fancy laces while she made her purchases.

"I wonder," she whispered to Mitchell, "does the picturesque phrase 'bull in a china shop' have any meaning for you?"

"It does," he replied, "but I believe I prefer it to the sobering one of 'dead as a doornail.' "

"Point taken," the lady said.

By afternoon, when they returned to Cavendish Square tired, hungry, and just a bit out of sympathy with one another, Delia was pleased to find Conrad Holcomb waiting for them in his book room. "Good," he said without preamble, "you are here at last."

He bowed over Delia's hand, then bid her be seated. "I have apprised the secretary of all you told me, Miss Barrington, and have turned over to him the packet William gave you. It may interest you to know that the assassination plot comes as no surprise to his office. Furthermore, he has assured me that his operatives have everything in hand. The packet will, of course, be most valuable when the perpetrators of this plot are arrested and brought to trial for treason."

"And what of me?" she asked. "Will my testimony be needed at the trial?"

"The secretary thought not."

Delia sighed with relief, happy to know she need be concerned with the matter no longer.

"Also, my dear, the Secretary wishes me to express to you his deepest appreciation for your assistance in this matter. And someday soon, he hopes to pay his respects to you in person."

Delia felt the heat of embarrassment rush to her face, and she was pleased that her host dropped the subject entirely and ordered a nuncheon served in the dining room for his son and his guest. "I trust you will forgive me, my dear Miss Barrington, if I do not join you. Unfortunately, I must leave, for I have a meeting with the prime minister at three. If it were anyone other than Perceval, I would not hesitate to send around my regrets. As it is . . . well . . . You do understand."

"Of course I do, sir, and I beg you will not give it another thought. When duty calls, nothing is more important."

"You are very good. Be assured, my dear, that I would much prefer to remain here, so I might become better acquainted with such a brave young lady."

"Oh, but I am not at all—"

"Brave? Your pardon, my dear young lady, but I cannot allow you to be the judge of that."

Before she could protest further, he made her a very courtly bow, putting an end to the conversation. "Until we meet again, Miss Barrington, I bid you adieu."

The nuncheon was delicious, and both Mitchell and Delia partook fully of the meal, as though they had not seen food in days. Conrad Holcomb's chef was a celebrity among the *ton,* and he upheld his reputation by serving chicken stewed with mushrooms in Marsala wine, and side dishes of honeyed carrots and steamed asparagus. Delia could not resist an ample serving of a raspberry custard that fairly melted in her mouth, and while she enjoyed the sweet, Mitchell peeled and ate a succession house peach.

He declined the butler's offer of a glass of port, and as soon as they left the table, Delia suggested that he return her to her home. "Now that I have my two stalwart protectors, there can be no objection to my returning to Grosvenor Square."

"There can be," Mitchell said, "but experience has taught me not to waste my energy on battles that cannot be won."

The berlin had been sent back to Fernbourne House to fetch Lady Regina, so Mitchell saw Delia home in a hackney. While he gave instructions to the Bow Street Runners, that one was to guard the front door and one the garden entrance, Delia opened the entrance door and stepped into the vestibule. On the instant, she knew her staff had returned.

The marble floor shone, all signs of dust gone; the entire house smelled of freshly applied beeswax, and a vase of sunny yellow daffodils stood on the console table, as if welcoming the lady of the house. "Miss Cordelia," cried an elderly butler, who hurried up from the kitchen, a polishing cloth in one hand and a silver platter in the other. "Welcome home."

"Thank you, Struthers. It is good to see you again, and so very good to be back in Grosvenor Square."

"Yes, miss. We are all happy to be home."

As if on cue, the housekeeper and two housemaids hurried forward, all eager to tell their mistress how they had spent the past two months and to ask about dear Master Robbie. When the butler spied Mitchell at the door, he shooed the women back to the kitchen and begged the gentleman's pardon. "May I take your hat, sir?"

"Major Holcomb will not be staying," Delia said. She was about to offer him her hand and thank him for seeing her home, when she spied a thick, square card of invitation lying on the console table. Curious, she picked up the card, broke the seal, and read the contents.

"Oh, my," she said.

Instantly, Mitchell caught her hand. "What is it? Nothing bad, I hope."

She shook her head. "At least *I* do not think so. The honor of my presence is requested for tomorrow evening at nine, at the ball being hosted by Lord Leeland."

Since Delia would not agree to decline the invitation to Lord Leeland's ball, Mitchell insisted upon escorting her to the affair. She was more than happy to agree to his escort for that evening, but she refused to so much as answer the door to him on the day of the ball, insisting that it would require the entire day for her to get ready for such an important function.

After two month's absence from town, she was convinced that her hair, her nails, and her complexion were all in dire need of attention. To this end, she spent the better part of the afternoon with cucumber slices on her eyelids to reduce any possible puffiness, Denmark wash on her face to refine the skin, and an application of almond paste on her hands to help repair the damage done while being tossed about in moats and sleeping in horse barns.

After a leisurely soak in a hip bath, Delia allowed her maid to dress her hair in the Grecian style, with half a dozen ringlets spilling like a bunch of grapes from her crown. She had chosen an apricot-colored gown of Turin gauze, and though the gown was at least two years old, its Grecian-style draping was timeless and undeniably flattering to her figure.

Her looking glass told her she was more than presentable, but she waited with bated breath to see Mitchell's reaction. Would he think her handsome enough to take in on his arm? The instant he was shown into the withdrawing room, she got her answer. Not in words, but in the way he looked at her—his gaze intent, serious, as if he had never seen her before. He seemed to drink her in from her head to her toes, and when he had looked his fill, he exhaled loudly.

As usual, his appearance quite stole her breath away, for he was the handsomest man she had ever known. Attired for a ball, he wore knee breeches of gold satin, topped by a cream waistcoat and a forest green coat, and beneath his arm he carried a *chapeau bras.* "Sir, you look quite elegant."

If he heard the compliment, he gave no indication of it. "Please," he said, "will you not reconsider this foolishness and remain at home?"

Delia shook her head, making the ringlets dance across the back of her neck. "I cannot. Somehow, I feel I must go, to see this through to the end."

Lord Leeland lived in rooms on Chesterfield Street, but the ball was being held at number seven Park Lane, at the home of his friend, Mr. Charles Vickers, a nabob newly returned from India. The town house was quite large, probably twice the size of Delia's home, and it had been recently renovated, appointed with chandeliers of Venetian crystal, silk wall coverings from China, and floors of the finest Italian marble. Delia had never before been inside the house, but the moment she crossed the threshold, she realized the layout was hauntingly familiar.

"Mitchell," she whispered. "This house—"

"Shh," he cautioned her. "I know what you are thinking."

Barely mouthing the words, she said, "This is the house depicted on the foolscap sketch from William's packet."

"Yes," he replied. "There can be no question of it."

As they joined the dozen or so people making their way up the grand staircase, Delia tried to recall where the doors and windows had been marked on the foolscap sketch. "If the two adjoining parlors are to the right," she whispered, "then the library where the dueling pistols are waiting must be to the left. Do you think there is any chance we could—"

"Shh," Mitchell warned again. "Whatever you are thinking, put it from your mind this instant, or I promise you, I will toss you over my shoulder and carry you from this place."

She was trying to think of some way to persuade him to help her look for the dueling pistols, when her attention was claimed by their lisping host. Resplendent in a lilac coat, silver waistcoat, and rose knee breeches, Lord Leeland stood out like a peacock beside a rather portly gentleman dressed entirely in black. The gentleman was unknown to Delia, but judging by his face, which had been turned quite leathery by continued exposure to the sun, she assumed he was the owner of the house. The India nabob.

"Mith Barrington," Lord Leeland said, "I am tho happy you could come. And Major Holcomb. Thith ith an unexpected pleathure, thir. Pray, allow me to make you known to Mithter Charlth Vickerth."

"Miss Barrington," Vickers said. "A pleasure to make your acquaintance."

Many times Delia had heard someone say their flesh crawled, but until that moment, she had not understood the sensation. The instant Charlth Vicketh touched her hand, she felt quite creepy, as if her skin had actually moved.

It was something in his eyes that made Delia want to give herself a good shake. They were the coldest blue she had ever seen. And though their owner smiled and said all that was expected of a welcoming host, one look into those chilling blue orbs was enough to convince Delia that this was the man who had written the letters in the packet.

A man with such eyes would not flinch at murder. Even the murder of a prince.

Thankfully for her composure, the press of guests was such that she and Mitchell were obliged to move on, so that others could pay their respects to their host. "Come," Mitchell said, offering her his arm, "let us join the dancers."

The double parlors were, indeed, to the right, and several dozen couples were already whirling about the brightly lit room to the music of an excellent string quartet. "Shall we?" Mitchell asked. As if fearing a negative reply, he took her firmly by the elbow and all but pushed her into the ballroom.

To keep from causing a scene, Delia did not pull away from his grasp. She could wait, for once he had received his allotted two dances and was obliged to relinquish her, she fully intended to find the library. There was no hurry, for it was only half past nine, and the Prince Regent would not arrive for at least another hour.

The thought had only just entered her mind when Delia heard some sort of stir belowstairs. She turned in time to see Lord Leeland hurry toward the top of the stairs, where guests were already pressing their backs against the walls in order to make way for the prince.

Someone signaled the string quartet to silence, and the entire room of dancers, realizing the significance, moved aside, making a path. "Is it he?" asked a giddy young miss. "I vow I shall faint if it is truly Prinny."

"I will thank you to remember," admonished her chaperon, "that His Royal Highness is not to be spoken of with such vulgar familiarity. And unless you wish to be taken home this instant, you will be so good as to keep your lips sealed and your eyes downcast, as befits a young lady fortunate enough to find herself in such exalted company."

"Yes, ma'am," the chastened chit replied.

Delia felt a moment of sympathy for the young,

inexperienced girl, and she wondered what the chaperon would say if she knew what was scheduled to happen in this so-called exalted company.

"Your Royal Highness," Lord Leeland said, bowing before a large gentleman wearing a royal blue domino that swept the floor, and a satin mask that covered the upper portion of his plump face. "We are honored by your presence, sire."

The large gentleman extended two pudgy, be-ringed fingers, which he withdrew an instant before his lordship could touch them, then he walked right past Mr. Charles Vickers and strolled toward the ballroom, inclining his head slightly in gracious acknowledgment of the bows and curtsies of the guests.

While the string quartet played "God Save the King," Delia heard murmurs in the crowd, speculation that the prince must mean to attend a masked ball later. It made sense, for it was not at all unusual for the Prince Regent to honor more than one party in an evening. Still, something about his costume made Delia uneasy. Why wear the domino and mask this early? Such cover-ups could not be all that comfortable, especially in this overheated ballroom.

With all eyes on the royal guest, Lord Alvanley stepped forward, bowed, then offered his arm to the prince. "Your Royal Highness," he said, "I beg you will be so good as to give an old friend a moment of your time?"

The prince nodded, still without uttering a word, and he and his friend, Lord Alvanley, exited through a door just behind the string quartet.

"How very odd," said the young girl who had been admonished to keep her lips sealed. For her impertinence, the chit received a rather vicious pinch on the arm from her chaperon, but Delia quite agreed with the girl's assessment. It was exceedingly odd for the Prince Regent, usually a very genial person, to practically snub the host whose party he had deigned to attend, then to enter a ballroom and exit it without at least exchanging a few pleasantries with his closest friends.

When Delia turned to voice her bewilderment to Mitchell, the sternness of his expression caused the words to remain unspoken on her lips. "What is it?" she asked.

"I am not certain," he said. "But if what I suspect is true, the action is about to commence, and I want you out of here. Now."

He put his arm around her shoulders and, with unseemly speed, led her from the ballroom and back toward the grand staircase. Unfortunately, those guests who had graciously moved aside for the Prince Regent were now being shoved aside by at least a dozen soldiers and fully that many nonuniformed men, all of them with pistols in hand.

Of their host and the nabob, there was no sign.

With their host disappearing and armed men pushing and shoving their way up the stairs, it was not to be wondered at that someone in the crowd screamed. Naturally, one scream led to another, and in seconds sheer chaos reigned, with the guests now shoving one another in their haste to get back down the stairs and out of the house.

Delia, realizing they would never make it through the panicked guests, suggested they find the servants' stairs.

"Good thinking," Mitchell said.

As they hurried down the newly carpeted corridor, past the private rooms, a series of shouted commands sounded from the ground floor, followed by at least two pistol shots.

"Halt!" someone shouted. "In the name of the law!"

Delia and Mitchell had almost reached the back stairs when a door was snatched open and Charles Vickers rushed out, a valise in his hand. When he saw them, he drew a pistol from inside his coat. "Stay back," he said, "or I will shoot."

From belowstairs, another shot rang out, and the nabob's leathery face went ashen. "How . . . how did this happen?" he muttered. Obviously not expecting an answer, he turned and ran down the stairs.

"Inside," Mitchell ordered, pushing Delia into the room Vickers had just left.

When he did not follow her, Delia knew he meant to pursue Charles Vickers. "Please," she begged, "do not go."

"Do not worry," he said, "just get on the floor and keep your head down. When bullets start flying, one never knows where they will hit."

He was already halfway down the stairs by the time Delia closed the door. She was about to do as he suggested and get down on the floor, when she realized she was in the library, the room she had hoped to find earlier.

It was an elegant apartment with teak shelves lining two of the walls—shelves holding hundreds of books, some of the volumes so new Delia fancied she could still smell the printer's ink. A fire burned brightly in the polished granite fireplace, and candles had been lit in each of the six wall sconces.

On the third wall, a landscape painting that had been mounted on piano hinges had been pushed aside, and the wall safe the painting hid stood open. Whatever valuables may have once been kept inside that receptacle, they were gone now, all save an etched crystal egg containing a four-leaf clover.

Delia went to the safe and removed the crystal egg, feeling its cool weight in her hand. She wondered why the good luck piece had been left behind. Could it be because the owner's luck had gone bad? She certainly hoped so.

She wondered as well if the empty safe had anything to do with the valise the nabob had been carrying.

She had little time to consider the matter, for someone spoke her name. "Miss Barrington," a man said. "What a fortuitous meeting."

Startled, she turned toward the far end of the room, where a slender gentleman in a lilac coat and rose knee breeches stood beside a handsome mahogany desk.

"Lord Leeland!"

"Yes," he said, all signs of the pretentious lisp gone, "it is I."

An involuntary shudder went through Delia. To see the once-lisping popinjay and know that he was, in fact, a murderer was as disconcerting as watching a kitten turn into a roaring, man-eating lion.

"You know, Miss Barrington, your Major Holcomb spoke the truth. One never knows where a bullet will hit."

"He . . . he is not *my* Major Holcomb?"

Lord Leeland waved a dismissive hand. "My mistake. I thought . . . But no matter. Mistakes seem to be the order of the day."

Delia agreed wholeheartedly with that observation, for she had certainly erred by coming into this room. While she watched, his lordship removed something from atop the desk, then slowly raised his arm. In his hand he held a dueling pistol, and the weapon was pointed directly at her.

"It would appear, Miss Barrington, that I am to get a second chance to rid myself of your meddlesome presence. I missed you that day in the garden, but at this close range, I feel certain I shall meet with greater success."

Chapter Eighteen

*D*elia could not decide which frightened her most, having a pistol pointed directly at her or hearing the hatred in Lord Leeland's voice. If the dueling pistol was the antique mentioned in the letter from the packet, such weapons were notorious for firing at the least pressure, she prayed his lordship had a steady hand. If she could keep him talking, perhaps Mitchell would return before the maniac decided to pull the trigger.

"So," she said, "it was you I heard in the garden at Fernbourne."

"It was. I cannot teli you how surprised I was to see you at Lady Regina's card party, alive and well."

"Thanks in part to the inefficiency of the two men you sent to Ems Regis."

"Yes," he said, "they were a regrettable choice. Two of Charles's men, actually. And when I realized the fools had failed to dispose of you, I decided to take matters into my own hands. It was most obliging of you to go for a walk in the garden."

"And most obliging of you, my lord, to be such a poor shot."

"You stupid, stupid girl!"

Though Delia knew she was treading on dangerous ground, she was glad to know she had wounded his

male pride. If she thought for a minute she could hit
him, she would throw the crystal egg she still held and
wound something a bit more tangible.

"Even now," he continued, "I find it difficult to
believe that one stupid woman could have been the
cause of so much trouble. We had everything planned
so well, Charles and I. Down to the last detail. A well-
choreographed dance, as it were."

"Not so well planned, I think. After all, William
Holcomb was able to discover your plot."

His lordship muttered a particularly vile oath, then
swung his free arm, knocking a brace of candles from
the desk. Delia gasped, but with that one burst of
temper, his anger seemed to subside, and when he
spoke again, his voice was oddly quiet, as if he were
talking to himself, trying to make sense of what had
happened, how their plan had gone wrong.

"We had the prince within our aim," he said. "All
we had to do was follow the plan, and ultimately we
would have been wealthy beyond our wildest dreams.
Never again would I have been a last-minute guest to
make up the numbers at table for some dull-witted
hostess. And I could have purchased a house like this.
No more living in bachelor's rooms. I would have been
a person of importance, a man of substance, a—"

"It was not the Prince Regent," Delia said.

Lord Leeland stared at her, confusion in his eyes,
as if he had just awakened from a trance. "What did
you say?"

"The man in the domino and mask, he was not
Prinny. He was an impostor. Probably one of the sec-
retary's men from the Home Department. I admit that
I did not see through the charade at first, but after—"

"Not the prince."

Lord Leeland made a sound that might have been
mistaken for a laugh, had his eyes not remained dull,
lifeless. "There is irony for you, that the guest of

honor should be an impostor. For as it happens, Charles was not the man I thought him to be either. No, not at all the reliable fellow I believed him to be."

He looked at Delia as if he expected some sort of commiseration from her for his having been deceived. "This was all his idea, don't you know. Until the nabob began filling my ears with his grand schemes, I was quite content with my little supply enterprise. I had a little something to live on—not much mind you, but enough—and no one got hurt."

Delia felt sick to her stomach. The man actually believed that cheating soldiers who were fighting to defend their country, depriving them of needed food and medical supplies, caused no harm.

"The plans to expand the operation were his. The nabob's! The *brave* India nabob, with his shipping connections and his band of cutthroats. All we had to do was insure that the Prince did not dissolve the present government and replace the men who were in my pay."

His lordship's mouth twisted into a sneer. "I cannot believe I was so deceived in Charles. Brave? Why, he was nothing of the sort. The moment he saw the soldiers, he turned and fled."

"Like a rat deserting a sinking ship?" Delia suggested.

His lordship was beyond hearing any voice but his own. "And he took the money. All of it. A third of it was mine. We were to divide it evenly; he and that detestable little murderer and I. But Charles would not hear reason. When I followed him to this room, and begged him not to leave without me, he pulled a pistol on me. Threatened to shoot me if I tried to follow him."

Apparently lost in recollection of the betrayal, he seemed to forget there was anyone else in the room. When the arm holding the pistol began to sag, Delia started inching toward the door.

"Stop!" he said, raising his arm once again. "Do not move. I have not forgotten that this is all your fault."

Her fault! Delia could not believe he actually blamed her for his present predicament.

It was obvious the man was losing his hold on reality, and Delia knew she must do something immediately or he would shoot her. If only she had a weapon of some sort. Something more substantial than the silly crystal egg, with its four-leaf clover, that unlucky good luck charm.

His lordship took careful aim. "Farewell, Miss Barrington. No doubt, I shall see you in hell."

He pulled back the hammer of the dueling pistol, and Delia, with nothing to lose, threw the crystal egg at him. She did not hit him, of course, that would have been too much to expect, but apparently instinct made him duck, and when he did, the weapon fired of its own accord. Thankfully, the bullet missed Delia entirely and lodged harmlessly in one of the unread books on the shelf behind her.

At the sound of the shot, the door burst open and Mitchell rushed in. "Delia!"

"Look out!" she yelled. "There is a second pistol on the desk."

Mitchell and Lord Leeland both dove for the pistol, and though his lordship reached it first, Mitchell was there in the next instant. He grabbed the smaller man's arm, and in one smooth motion twisted it around behind Leeland's back.

The slender peer was no match for a man of Mitchell Holcomb's size and strength, and he dropped the weapon. "Stop! Stop!" he yelled. "Please, do not hurt me. I cannot endure pain."

"Now there's a shame," Mitchell said, kicking the pistol out of reach, "for you've more than a little pain coming to you. And I so wanted to give you a sample of what I gave your friend Vickers when I caught up with him."

With that, Mitchell drew back his fist and hit the man solidly in the stomach. "That one is for my cousin." He hit him another solid blow that caused him to double over completely. "And that one is for the anguish you caused Miss Barrington."

He did not hit him a third time. There was no need, for the man who would have murdered a monarch lay at Mitchell's feet, retching and moaning, a threat no longer, just a pathetic little man in lilac satin.

Chapter Nineteen

*D*elia and Mitchell had hoped to set out for Ems Regis the morning following the ball. Unfortunately, it was not to be. There were interviews to be got through with the authorities, and eyewitness identifications of Georgie and his pal, who had been arrested prior to the ball.

The man who murdered William still had not been apprehended, and though Delia was not certain she would ever feel truly safe, not as long as that villain remained free, she chose to dismiss the two Bow Street Runners, explaining that they made her feel like a prisoner. "Besides," she added, hoping with all her heart that what she said was true, "chances are the murderer has found a hole somewhere and crawled into it. Especially if he has heard about the arrests of his employers."

Mitchell was not convinced, but he agreed to the dismissal of the Runners. After all, he and Delia were bound for West Sussex to retrieve William's son and take him to his grandfather, at Holcomb Park. Surely he could keep Delia safe while at his uncle's estate.

With all the demands on their time, it was two full days before Delia and Mitchell were ready to leave town. Once again Lady Regina lent them her well-sprung berlin, and her ladyship and her husband drove to Grosvenor Square with their son to wish the travelers Godspeed.

"Take care of yourself," Conrad Holcomb said as he helped Delia into the carriage. "And when you arrive at Holcomb Park, be so good as to convey my regards to my brother."

"Yes," Lady Regina said, "and when you have time, my dear Delia, I beg you to send word by post, telling us of Sir Allistair's reaction upon meeting his grandson. I want to know every detail, for I am confident the boy is just what my brother-in-law needs to lift him out of his present melancholy."

"I shall send a letter immediately, ma'am."

When the good-byes were at an end and the carriage wheels rattled over the cobblestone streets, taking the berlin out of London and due south, Delia thought about that promise to write. She would, of course, honor her word, but judging by her present despondency, writing that letter would probably tear her heart right out of her chest.

Each time she thought of the moment when she would actually surrender the little boy to his grandfather, a painful lump lodged in her throat, making swallowing difficult. How was she to bear the pain of parting with the child she had come to love?

Worse yet, how was she to survive the agony of parting with Mitchell, the man she loved more deeply with each breath she took? Like her, once they delivered Robbie to Holcomb Park, Mitchell would return to his own life—a life that did not include Delia.

She had known Major Mitchell Holcomb less than a fortnight, yet in that time he had taken over her heart, her soul, her every thought. She had never dreamed she could love a man as passionately, as completely as she loved Mitchell, and after tomorrow, she might never see him again.

During the nearly sixty-mile drive to Ems Regis, Delia and Mitchell spoke very little. There was so much she wanted to say, and the enormity of what she dare not mention rendered her practically tongue-tied. *By the way, Mitchell, did I happen to mention that I love you with a passion that completely over-whelms me, and that it is my heart's desire to spend the rest of my life with you?*

Ha! She could just imagine what a conversation starter that would be! That is, if her beloved did not jump from the moving coach on the instant and disappear, never to be seen or heard from again.

"At least the road is clear," Mitchell said.

As a conversational gambit, it lacked real sparkle, but at least it was a start. "And dry," Delia said, offering her own scintillating mite.

Moments passed before he spoke again.

"No high tide to detain us this time."

"No, not at this hour. If I remember correctly, the times of the high and low tides progress roughly an hour per day. Noon and midnight one day, one and one the next, and so on."

"Ah, yes," he said.

Another silence stretched between them. "So," he said finally, "judging by the tide that detained us five days ago, we need have no concern until some time in the early evening."

"Around nine, I should think." Not that Delia was concerned. Chances were, she would be in her room at Sky Cottage by that hour, crying into her pillow at the knowledge of the heart-wrenching separations the next day would bring.

"By the way," Mitchell said, "should we ask Nadja Eskew to come with us to Holcomb Park?"

Delia shook her head. "She and I discussed that possibility several weeks ago, when I planned to take Robbie to his grandfather by myself. Nadja's life is at Sky Cottage, and just as she knew her daughter's and her granddaughter's rightful places were in London, she knows that Robbie's fate lies with Sir Allistair. As his grandfather's heir, the child will need to grow up on the estate."

"She is very wise."

"I do hope, though, that Sir Allistair will see fit to allow Robbie to visit his great-grandmother from time to time. Nadja loves the boy very much. He is all the family she has left, and you cannot know how alone one feels with no family . . . no one to love."

To Delia's surprise, Mitchell reached across and took her hand. "I think Nadja is not the only one who loves the child. Surely you will wish to see him as well?"

The slight roughness of Mitchell's palm against her skin sent frissons of delight all the way up Delia's arm. When he turned her hand over and began making small circles with his thumb on the inside of her wrist, the delight spread throughout her body, making it difficult for her to think of anything but Mitchell, and what he was doing to her. "Of . . . of course," she muttered, trying to remember his last question. "Robbie is very dear to me."

"And Nadja?" he asked softly. "Is she dear to you as well?"

If he did not cease that sweet torture and release her hand, she would go insane! "I have grown quite fond of Nadja Eskew, if that is what you mean."

He seemed to ponder her remarks. "Let me see, now, if I understand the situation. You love Robbie, and you are fond of the boy's great-grandmother as well, so that there is every likelihood you will wish to visit each of them from time to time."

What was he getting at?

"It is unfortunate," he said, releasing her hand and sitting back against the squabs, for all the world as if he had never touched her, "that you do not keep a carriage. The journey from London to Sussex is so much more comfortable if one has one's own equipage."

"Yes," she said, more confused than ever at his purpose in this very odd conversation. "I daresay you are right. One's own carriage must always be preferable to a hired chaise."

"But not, I think, preferable to living within a somewhat easier traveling distance. Which brings to mind something I had meant to mention earlier. Do you not think it would be easier if, say, you resided at—"

"Ems Regis!" the coachman called down to them. "You want I should stop at the village, Major? Or shall I continue to the cottage?"

Mitchell muttered something under his breath, as if annoyed by the interruption, then he leaned out the window so he could call up to the man on the box. "Continue to the cottage," he said.

For the next few minutes, further conversation was impossible, for the coachman failed to slow the team, and the berlin bounced over the narrow sandy lane like a ship in a rough sea, tossing the passengers back and forth. Delia was obliged to hold on to the strap with both hands just to keep from being thrown to the floor of the carriage. And as if that were not enough, the nuncheon of prawns and wild rice she and Mitchell had shared at the Blue Cockerel Inn less than an hour ago threatened to play her false at any moment.

Outside, the yellow gorse, the tall, spindly sea grasses, even the post bearing the small wooden sign that read "Sky Cottage," seemed to bounce past the carriage window like weird India rubber balls, adding further to Delia's physical distress. By the time the coachman finally reined in the horses beside the ten-foot hedge, Delia's stomach was rolling, her head ached, and she was much too happy at the discontinuation of motion to think of anything else.

Not Robbie. Not Nadja Eskew. And not even the object of Mitchell's interrupted remarks about her future place of residence.

The flint and mortar cottage just beyond the hedge appeared to be undulating slowly before Delia's eyes, and even when her feet touched solid ground, it was several seconds before the cottage ceased its wavy dance.

To her relief, she did not embarrass herself by casting up her accounts, but she felt no great confidence that the danger was passed. "I . . . I think I need to go to my room," she said.

Mitchell was in the process of giving the coachman a tongue-lashing for the wild ride, but he took one look at Delia and scooped her up into his arms. He did not stop in the main room, but continued up the narrow stairs leading to the upper floor. Only when he reached her bedchamber and kicked open the door did he recall the disarray left there by Georgie and his malicious knife.

"Damnation!"

After setting Delia on her feet, Mitchell tossed what remained of the savagely gutted mattress onto the wooden bed, then covered it with the quilt he found in the corner room. "Here," he said, helping her to sit, then removing her spencer and her bonnet so she might lie back more comfortably. "I will find Nadja, and have her make you some of her tea."

"Nadja will not be here."

"What?"

"She was to remain with her people until she saw my signal that it was safe to return to the cottage."

Though it made Delia's head swim to do so, she glanced around the room until she spied Nadja's kerchief lying among the feathers from the mattress. "The *diklo*, over there. I was to hang it in the window. Nadja said someone would be watching."

Mitchell fetched the kerchief and promised to hang it immediately. "For now, all you need to think about is getting some rest."

*   *   *

Though she had not expected to do so, Delia slept for several hours, and when she awoke, she felt her old self again. Someone, Mitchell she supposed, had brought up her valise and set a candle and a pitcher of fresh water on the washstand. Thanking him silently for his consideration, she washed her face and combed her hair, then took the candle and made her way belowstairs.

While she had slept, Mitchell had been a busy fellow, for the furniture in the downstairs room had been straightened and the drawers returned to the dresser in the kitchen area, making the room appear almost normal again. As well, a fire blazed in the fireplace. Of the miracle worker himself, there was no sign.

Delia remembered hearing Mitchell ask the coachman if he would prefer to remain at Sky Cottage or to find a room at the small inn in the village. The servant had chosen the latter, and Delia assumed that Mitchell had gone there as well, to procure a meal. She was not the least bit hungry, but she felt stiff from inactivity. Since there was nothing to keep her at the cottage, she decided to fetch her shawl and go out-of-doors for a breath of fresh air.

If she walked toward the village, there was a good chance she would meet Mitchell on his way back to the cottage. Such an opportunity was not to be missed, for after tomorrow, when they journeyed to Sir Allistair's estate, there was no knowing if she would ever again be alone with the man she loved.

For all she knew, tonight would be all the time she had left with him, and she did not want to waste a moment of it.

Mitchell had not told her his plans. It was possible that he meant to remain with his uncle for a sennight or more. Or, he might wish to return to Fernbourne House right away, in which case he would probably

send Delia back to London in the berlin. If he provided her with an extra outrider, that would more than
satisfy any obligation on his part.

At the thought of returning to London alone, she
was obliged to subdue a sob. "Do not start weeping,"
she warned herself. "Not now." There would be time
enough for weeping when she was back in Grosvenor
Square, wondering how she would get through the
days, the months, the years, without Mitchell.

Determined to make the most of what might prove
to be her last private moments with him, she tossed
the shawl around her shoulders, left the cottage, and
began walking toward Ems Regis, crossing her fingers
that she would meet him. Chance was a fine thing, but
Delia was a woman with a mission, and if need be,
she was prepared to wait near the old bridge for hours,
or however long it took Mitchell to decide to come
home.

The night air was fresh and crisp, with a breeze
blowing in from the Channel, bringing its decidedly
briny aroma. The moon was high in the sky, and
though it was a waning moon, it shone bright and
silvery, casting a soft light on the hedge, the ground,
and the few trees, making a lantern unnecessary.

In the two months she had stayed at Sky Cottage,
Delia had walked to the village only once. Of course,
her previous ramble had been during daylight hours,
but she had little fear of getting lost . . . or of getting
in trouble. This route led directly to the village, and
even at high tide she was safe as long as she did not
wander far from the lane.

Mitchell had thought much the same thing earlier
that evening, when he and his father's coachman had
walked to the village. They could hear the tide coming
in, and the servant had expressed some concern. "I
b'aint much of a one for swimming, Major."

"There is no need for concern," Mitchell informed

him. "The village proper does not flood, only the low-lying area surrounding it. Therefore, if we stay on the path, we have nothing to fear."

The coachman had helped straighten the vandalized cottage and bring in wood for the fire, and in appreciation for his assistance, Mitchell had offered to stand the man a tankard of ale. The coachman had smacked his lips in pleasurable anticipation, and the two men had gone in search of a tavern.

That had been more than an hour ago, and now Mitchell was returning from the tavern alone. All along the high street the one- and two-story shops were closed and dark. Apparently, most of the citizens were safe in their beds for the night, and as a consequence, Mitchell was the only person about.

Or so he thought.

He still had to cross the narrow wooden bridge that spanned the ravine. It was the only way to enter or leave the village proper, and because he did not trust the rickety old collection of boards and pilings, he made certain he watched where he put his feet. The wood was damp from the incoming waves that slapped noisily against the piers that supported the abutment, and though he could not see beneath the bridge, he knew the water was rising. One false step and he would be in serious trouble.

Because he was concentrating on getting across the bridge and not on what was in front of him, Mitchell still thought he was alone. He discovered his mistake when a strange-looking little man suddenly stepped out of the shadows. "Yer pardon, Guv'nor," the man said, "but happen ye could help me. I'm looking for a place called Sky Cottage."

Delia had just turned off the lane when she saw a man crossing the bridge. It was Mitchell. He was a good fifty yards away, but she knew it was him. If his height and the width of his powerful shoulders had not given him away, the sudden fierce pounding of her heart would have convinced her that coming toward her was the man who owned that life-sustaining organ . . . lock, stock, and barrel.

She stopped where she was, deciding to wait for him to join her. Just the thought of being on that rickety old bridge, while the ravine beneath filled with water, made her knees quake with fright, and she did not want to take the chance of startling Mitchell by calling out to him.

As well, if she remained quietly where she was, she could watch him without the embarrassment of his knowing she watched. He moved with such grace, such confidence, such joy, as though he was happy to be alive, and intelligent enough to realize that being alive was a gift not to be squandered.

He had made his way across the bridge, and she was about to call to him when a man dressed in black, from his coat down to his tasseled Hessians, stepped out of the shadows into the bright moonlight. At sight of that man, Delia's heart jumped into her throat.

No! she thought. It cannot be him!

And yet, it was.

She had seen him only once in her life, when he murdered William Holcomb in cold blood, but if she lived to be a hundred, she would never forget him. He was actually a rather nondescript man, slightly stoop-shouldered and not especially large, but he was a heartless killer, and such men made indelible impressions.

For two months Delia had lived in fear, convinced that this villain would find her. And now, just when she decided that he had taken himself off and had forgotten all about her, here he was. He was talking to Mitchell, and Mitchell had no idea that the man before him was a murderer.

She had to warn him. But how? How could she tell him to beware without letting the murderer know she was there?

Without a doubt, the villain had come to kill her, and every instinct told her to hide, not to make a sound lest he hear her. But what if he hurt Mitchell? What if he tried to kill her beloved?

The very thought made Delia physically ill. She could not let Mitchell be hurt. She loved him too much. If something happened to him and she could have prevented it, she would not want to live.

If one of them must die, let it be her.

She was never to know at what point her love for Mitchell Holcomb overcame her fear of the murderer, but she suddenly found herself licking her lips, then pursing them. Moments later, the tune she whistled carried through the night air.

Mitchell could not believe his ears. Someone was whistling, and if he knew anything of the matter, the whistler was Delia. But what the deuce was she doing here?

This strange little man had just stepped out of the shadows and asked for directions to Sky Cottage, and as Mitchell was about to ask him what business he had at the cottage, he heard Delia whistle.

Like any soldier worth his salt, Mitchell had learned to trust his instincts, and though he had no idea what was going on here, some sixth sense told him to beware. It told him as well that he damned well better remember that tune . . . and fast!

He knew the song, though at the moment it was merely teasing the edges of his memory. He had not heard it in years, but he knew it. Think, he told himself. Think.

The odd little man turned to look behind him, presumably to see who was whistling, and as he did so, he slipped his hand inside his coat, as if reaching for a weapon.

On the instant, Mitchell remembered the name of the song. It was a hymn long out of favor, and it was called "Behold the Face of Evil."

Chapter Twenty

"*B*ehold the Face of Evil."

Had he come face-to-face with evil? He trusted Delia, if she said he was in the presence of evil, then it was so.

The man from the shadows had put his hand in his coat, and now, when he pulled it out, it held a pistol. "So, missy," he said, backing away so that he was out of Mitchell's immediate reach, "ye know who I am, do ye? I thought ye might remember my face. Now, suppose ye come on over here, just a bit closer, where I can see *yer* face. I want a good look at the person who come between me and enough money to make me rich. And I want to watch ye when I put a bullet through yer—"

"Delia," Mitchell said, stepping between her and the pistol, "stay where you are."

He walked toward the man, who backed away until he was standing on the bridge. "Keep yer distance," he said, "I'd as soon shoot two as one."

"Really? Go ahead, then, you murdering little weasel."

"Mitchell, no!"

She had only just yelled when the pistol fired and Mitchell grabbed his shoulder. He reeled slightly, but he managed to remain upright. "Now you have but one shot left," he said, "and I am not dead yet."

As if a bullet in the shoulder was no more than a flea bite, he lunged at the man in black, grabbing for the weapon. Ordinarily, such an unevenly matched fight would have been over within a matter of seconds, but Mitchell was wounded, and it was an indication of how badly he was hurt that he did not dispense with the fellow in one telling blow.

As it was, he only just managed to wrench the pistol from the man's grasp. After tossing the weapon aside, he used his fist to hit the man squarely in the face. It was a powerful blow, one that brought the man to his knees; unfortunately, the force of the swing nearly knocked Mitchell off balance as well.

While Mitchell tried to right himself, the man got to his feet, all the while cursing and snarling like some sort of wild animal. "I'll kill ye for that!"

Filled with fury, he ran at Mitchell, head down, and butted him in the stomach. Just as he made contact, however, Mitchell brought the heel of his hand down, hitting the man between his shoulder blades. Both men went down.

While Delia watched in horror, they struggled, rolling first one way then the next on the slippery bridge. It was obvious that neither of them realized how close they were to the edge. Delia realized it, however, and as she watched, terror filling her senses, she prayed that Mitchell would be saved.

For a moment it looked as if her prayer had been answered, for the pounding and the grunting stopped, and Mitchell began struggling to stand, while the smaller man lay on his back, unmoving. "Oh, thank heaven," she said.

She was about to run to Mitchell, who had finally made it all the way to his feet, when the murderer moved suddenly. In one surprising maneuver, he thrust his legs between Mitchell's ankles, then immediately twisted onto his right side. Mitchell was caught completely off guard. Though he flailed his arms

about, trying to maintain his balance, he lost the
battle.

As Mitchell pitched headfirst over the side of the
bridge, the murderer laughed like one crazed. His jub-
ilance was short-lived, however, for as if by some
stroke of justice, the tassel of his left Hessian had
become hung in the fold-over of Mitchell's right top
boot. And though the little man grabbed the edge of
the bridge, holding on for dear life, Mitchell's weight
pulled him over the side as well.

As the villain lost his hold on the slippery wood,
his face registered complete shock, as though he could
not believe that he, too, might die. Just before he hit
the roiling water, he screamed, the sound so feral it
defied description.

Or was it Delia who screamed?

She was not sure. All she knew for certain was that
Mitchell was in the water, and that even excellent
swimmers often did not survive the force of the rising tide.

Completely forgetting her own fear of the rickety
wooden structure and the potentially deadly water
below, she ran forward and fell on her knees, looking
over the side of the bridge for any sign of Mitchell.
She called his name repeatedly, but there was no answer, only the pounding of the waves against the sides
of the ravine and against the pilings that supported
the bridge abutments.

Delia's breath caught in her throat, for some large,
dark object was being dashed against the pilings, time
and again. Like some giant puppet whose handler had
dropped the strings, it was being thrown about by the
waves, yet it offered no resistance.

For one brief second, that object swept beneath
Delia, and she saw the deathly white face, the eyes
open but no longer seeing. It was the murderer. He
must have broken his neck when he fell, for his head
was at a most unnatural angle.

Terrified that Mitchell may have met a similar fate, Delia ran to the edge of the ravine where she could look beneath the bridge. To her relief, Mitchell was there, just out of her reach. The back of his coat was caught on one of the splintered pilings, and though his arms and legs were being tossed about by the rising tide, his head was still above water.

"Mitchell! Mitchell, can you hear me?"

When he did not answer, her heart all but stopped. Thankfully, before that organ failed her completely, she heard him moan. He was alive! Unconscious, but alive. Now all she had to do was run to the village and get help.

She had no more than thought of running, when a wave slapped Mitchell in the face. The water was still rising! What if she could not find help in time, and Mitchell drowned? She had no idea how long it took to drown, but she had heard it was a very swift death.

Afraid to take the chance on leaving, she begged heaven for help. "Please," she prayed. "What am I to do?"

This was her worst nightmare come true. Mitchell had stepped between her and the murderer to save her life, and now she must do something to save him. But what? He was the hero, not her. He was a brave soldier, while she—

Mitchell moaned again, and in that instant Delia knew that no matter how frightened she was, she was not going to let Mitchell drown. Not as long as she had breath in her body.

She was not brave, but neither was she stupid. All she needed to do was think. To find some way to keep Mitchell's head above water until the tide went back out, and at the same time, keep herself from drowning.

Mitchell was fortunate that he had been caught by the splintered wood of the piling; otherwise, his fate might have been the same as the killer's.

The piling! That was it! If she could secure herself

to the piling, she would not be swept away, and she could hold Mitchell's head up out of the water. But how was she to—

Before the question had formed completely in her mind, she knew the answer. She knew what to do.

As the plan took shape in her brain, an almost eerie calm settled on her. It was as if heaven, or her intense concentration, had pushed all other thoughts and sensations aside. She had but one thought. One purpose. One objective.

She removed her shawl and clamped it firmly between her teeth to keep it secure; then, while holding to the edge of the bridge, she eased her way down the muddy ravine, one tiny step at a time, until she could wrap one leg around the abutment just above Mitchell's head. Telling herself not to look down, she moved ever closer until finally she straddled the abutment like a horse, her feet swinging in midair.

So far, so good. Except for the fact that the spray from the water was turning her fingers icy cold, she felt reasonably secure.

With her knees pressing tightly against the sides of the abutment, she leaned forward and passed one end of the shawl beneath and around the thick, square timber, then tied it in a knot. The other end of the shawl she tied around her waist. Then, as Mitchell had done when they were at the moat, she lowered herself into the water.

The piling was only a matter of inches from her, so she was beside Mitchell in a matter of seconds. Though the rushing water made the task more difficult than she had expected, she wrapped both her legs and her right arm around the piling, then used her left arm to lift Mitchell's face out of the water.

She had no idea how long she clung to that piling, but by the time a pair of local men came from the tavern and staggered across the bridge, she was so cold she could no longer feel her legs. She could still yell, however, and yell she did.

Thankfully, the men were not totally inebriated, and they investigated the shouts coming from beneath the bridge. "Gor blimey!" one of them said.

"Zounds!" said the other. "Just how drunk am I?"

"Not so far gone that you're imagining things. Now, fetch some help, you foolish old sot!"

"Right you are. I'll try the innkeeper."

While the first man stayed behind to offer encouragement, his friend weaved his way back to the inn to get help.

Soon Delia heard at least a half dozen men coming at a run, and within a very short time she and Mitchell were wrapped in blankets and sitting before the inn fire, drinking cups of hot tea laced with brandy. If their rescuers crowded around a bit too close and stared at the bedraggled pair as though they were a raree-show, Delia offered no objection. Let them look their fill; they had earned it.

At that moment, all she cared about was that Mitchell was alive and that she had not failed him.

They stayed at the inn for the remainder of the night, but by mid-morning of the next day, Mitchell declared himself ready to leave his bed. The bullet had passed through his shoulder, and by some stroke of good luck, it had done no permanent damage.

The local apothecary had cleaned and bandaged the wound the night before, and that morning he returned to check on the patient. "My advice, Major Holcomb, is that you remain in bed for at least another two days. After that, if you will keep your arm in a sling for at least two weeks, and see your physician as soon as you return to town, I see no reason why you should suffer any ill effects from the injury.

"You will have a scar, of course, but since it will

not be your first, I doubt you will give it a thought. Not an old soldier like you."

Mitchell agreed that another scar was of little consequence, but that was all he agreed to. He flatly refused to remain at the inn. When no amount of argument would dissuade him, Delia gave up the attempt and said they would return that day to Sky Cottage.

Escorted by the coachman and at least a dozen curious villagers, they walked down the high street toward the bridge. When they reached that infamous structure, everyone paused, as if a moment of solemnity was in order. The body of the murderer had not yet been found, but Delia could not find it in her heart to utter a prayer for his soul. The man had murdered William Holcomb and nearly succeeded in killing Mitchell, and as far as she was concerned, he could roast in the fires of hell.

It was low tide, and a mere trickle of water remained in the ravine. As Delia looked at the now innocuous liquid shimmering with the sun's rays, it was difficult to believe that mere hours ago it had been a killer.

Almost as if he read her thoughts, Mitchell took her hand. They stood quietly for a moment, then he leaned close and whispered in her ear. "The first thing I do after we are married, is teach you to swim."

"Married!"

"Or," he said, giving her a smile so wicked it all but melted her bones, "I could teach you something else first—something I guarantee we will both enjoy enormously—and the swimming lessons could be second."

With so many people around, Delia could not ask Mitchell what he meant by speaking of marriage. If this was his way of repaying her for what happened beneath the bridge, she wanted no part of it. But if . . .

if . . . She dare not even think about the other possibility.

Naturally, she thought of nothing else! During their entire walk back to Sky Cottage, she was plagued by uncertainty, and all manner of questions chased one another around in her brain.

"After we are married."

Did he mean it? Was he merely teasing her? Had she misheard? And if she had not misheard, did he—could he possibly—love her?

"Pisliskurja Sedra," Nadja said the moment Delia entered the cottage. "Darling child. How are you?"

"I am well, *Phuri daj.*"

While the two women hugged, Mitchell studied Nadja Eskew, or "little mother," as Delia called her. She looked much as she had the last time he saw her, with her small, bare feet showing beneath a faded, ankle-length skirt, and numerous noisy bracelets *clinking* against one another at her wrists. When he looked at her this time, however, he saw not an old Gypsy whose motives he suspected, but a kindly old woman who had done everything in her power to protect her great-grandson and the woman who brought him to her.

Cordelia Barrington was nothing to Nadja Eskew, and yet the old woman had opened her heart to her. She called Delia her darling child, and for Delia's sake, she was willing to suspend all doubts about the angry soldier who had come in answer to a letter.

When Delia hurried up the stairs to see the child who napped in his cot, Nadja stared at Mitchell, almost as if she were looking inside his soul. "I am a *taibhsear,*" she said "a seer of visions, and I know that you have love in your heart for my little friend."

He did not dissemble. "I love her as I never thought to love any woman. I hope you do not disapprove."

"Dili! Imbecile! As if my approval is needed."

"Not needed, but certainly wanted."

Mollified, the old woman nodded. "You will make her happy. I have seen it in a vision."

Mitchell did not believe in seers and visions, but he was happy to know the old woman was willing to accept him.

"And now," she said, holding out her hand, "you still owe me two shillings for a night's lodging, plus an additional sixpence for the horses. No," she amended quickly, "twelve pence, for those highbred cattle of yours have done nothing but eat their heads off!"

Chapter Twenty-one

Saying good-bye to Nadja had been difficult, but journeying to Holcomb Park, to present Sir Allistair with his heretofore unknown grandson, had Delia so nervous she could barely swallow. All that kept her sane was the necessity of taking care of the little boy while in route. Not that an eight-month-old child was so very much trouble, but he had missed his nap, and he whined for the first part of the drive.

He had finally fallen asleep in Delia's arms, and when she spared a moment to look up at Mitchell, who sat opposite her, he was watching her as though he had never seen her before. "You will make a wonderful mother," he said softly.

Drat the man! Each time he spoke, he left her more confused than before. Annoyed more than she wished to admit, she felt her anger flair. "I doubt I shall ever be a mother."

"Oh?" he said, amusement in those marvelous gray eyes, "and why is that?"

"Because there is not a man in the entire world I would consider marrying."

To her surprise, he leaned forward, being careful not to wake the sleeping child, and kissed her. His mouth was warm, and his lips lingered on hers, moving ever so slowly until she thought she would swoon with the sweetness of it.

When he ended the kiss and sat back, he spoke as if nothing had occurred. "You were saying?"

"I . . . uh . . ."

He leaned forward once again, and his lips brushed first one corner of her mouth then the other. This time when he sat back, he said, "I interrupted you. Pray continue."

How could she continue when her mind had turned to mush? "Conversation takes two," she said, "and you . . . you are not doing your part."

"Forgive me," he said, then he leaned forward once again and claimed her lips in a kiss so soft, so sweet it made her feel as though she were drowning in ecstasy. Every inch of her body shimmered with pleasure, and when he moved away this time, she wanted to cry out to him to come back, to kiss her again.

"How was that for conversation?" he asked. "Did it tell you anything?"

Yes! No! She wanted to scream. Why was he tormenting her? If he loved her, why did he not tell her so. In words!

She was about to ask that very question when the carriage made a sharp turn to the left and passed through the entrance gates to Holcomb Park. "We are here," Mitchell said. "At last."

"Sir Allistair is in the morning room," the butler informed him. The elderly servant had been in service at Holcomb Park for more than forty years, and when he looked at the child in Delia's arms, his eyes grew so large he looked positively owlish.

"Shall I show the young lady into the silver drawing room, Major?"

Mitchell shook his head. "I think it will be best if Miss Barrington and the child wait in the little alcove next to the morning room, Pimstock, where they will be close at hand should my uncle wish to see them right away."

Though nothing more telling was said, the elderly servant's chin began to quiver. "I shall see that they are made comfortable, Major." His voice broke on the final word, and he had to excuse himself while he pulled a linen handkerchief from inside his coat. After he wiped his eyes, he looked again at Robbie. "Such a beautiful boy," he said, "and so very like—"

"No need to announce me," Mitchell said, "I do not think my uncle will mind."

"No, sir," Pimstock. "Not at all, sir."

Mitchell knocked at the door of the morning room, then let himself in, and as he closed the door, he heard the elderly butler begin to weep softly.

"Good day, uncle."

"Mitchell, my boy. How good of you to call."

There was a time when the master of Holcomb Park could be heard from one end of his house to the next, shouting orders and calling for his dogs or one of the servants. Now his voice sounded paper thin and frail, almost as if it pained him to speak.

At seventy-two, Sir Allistair was only five years older than Conrad Holcomb, but in the nearly three months since the death of his only son, the baronet had aged considerably, so much so that he now looked at least a dozen years older than his brother. His thick, gray hair was in sad need of cutting, his complexion was sallow, and his once lively blue eyes were dull, as if they had lost all hope of ever again seeing anything of interest.

Mitchell crossed to the fireplace, where the old gentleman sat, a shawl around his shoulders and a blanket across his lap. "My father sends his regards, uncle. As does my mother."

"They are both well?" Sir Allistair asked, his voice revealing little interest in the reply.

"They are in excellent health, sir, but it is not my parents I came here to discuss. I have come about another matter entirely."

When his uncle did not ask the nature of that matter, Mitchell reached inside his coat and removed the
letter that was to have come to Sir Allistair more than
two weeks ago. "This letter was meant for you, uncle,
written by Miss Cordelia Barrington, a young lady
who waits in the little alcove just outside this room. I
took the liberty of opening the missive, for which I
hope you will forgive me, but now I feel it is time
that you read it."

Sir Allistair took the letter, though without any
show of enthusiasm, and held it toward the firelight,
the better to see the words. He read slowly, his lips
moving slightly, so Mitchell was able to follow along,
almost as if reading the letter himself. Even had the
old gentleman's lips not moved, Mitchell would have
known when he came to the part about William having a wife, for Sir Allistair's hands began to tremble.

As his uncle continued to read, tears slipped down
his cheeks and fell unheeded upon the front of his
coat. "There is a child," he said. "My son had a child.
A boy."

He crushed the letter to his chest, almost as if he
were hugging the son he loved, then he closed his eyes
and laid his head back against the top of the chair.
"A child," he said. "I have a grandson."

After raking the back of his hand across his eyes to
swipe away the tears, he gave the letter back to Mitchell. "Read it aloud, my boy. All of it. Begin at the
beginning and do not leave out a single word."

When Mitchell had read the whole, his uncle hid
his face in his hands and wept unashamedly.

After a time, when Sir Allistair had managed to
compose himself, Mitchell asked if he wished to see
the marriage lines. "I assure you, they are authentic.
And there can be no question that Robbie is William's son."

"Robbie. The boy's name is Robert?"

"Yes, sir. Robert Allistair Holcomb."

A fresh supply of tears filled the old gentleman's eyes, but he brushed them away with an impatient hand. "And this young lady who wrote the letter, did you say she is here?"

"Yes, sir. In the little alcove. She and young Robbie. I believe Pimstock is with them."

Sir Allistair rose from his chair and hurried across the room, moving like a man suddenly reborn. When he opened the door, he paused just a moment and drew in a ragged breath. "Pimstock!" he yelled. "Where the deuce are you?"

"Here, Sir Allistair," the butler answered.

"Well, do not stand about like some noddy, bring me my grandson!"

While the sun sank below the horizon, leaving bold oranges and bright pinks smeared across the western sky, Delia sat on one of the small wrought-iron settees that were scattered about the park, watching the colors slowly fade into twilight. She had been there for the better part of an hour, not certain what to do with herself in an unfamiliar house, especially one that had been turned upside down, albeit happily so.

Feeling very much the interloper and not wanting to intrude upon Sir Allistair's privacy, she had thought it best to take herself outside. Soon she would have to return to the house, however, for with the sun gone, she was beginning to feel chilled.

"I brought you a shawl," Mitchell said, surprising her from her revery, and causing her to gasp.

"Your pardon," he said, "I did not mean to startle you."

"I was lost in thought."

He did not ask what she was thinking, nor if he might join her. He merely draped the shawl around her shoulders, then blithely wedged his large frame into the minimal space available on the wrought iron settee. When Delia complained that the settee was not actually meant for two, he told her not to worry, that he knew just how to give them a bit more room.

"There," he said, stretching his arm across the back of the seat, "is that not better?"

No! It was worse, far worse, for he was much too close.

Did he not realize that his firm thigh was pushing against hers, and that his muscular arm was practically draped across her shoulders? And his hand! How could he not know that his hand had worked its way beneath the shawl, and that it was now pressed against her upper arm?

He must know. And yet, when she looked at him, he seemed totally absorbed in watching the fading of the colors in the sky, apparently oblivious to how intimately his body was touching hers.

With Mitchell so close, Delia's senses were filled with the clean, masculine smell that was so much a part of him. The fragrance was causing a strange fluttering inside her chest, and making her long to nuzzle her face against the strong column of his throat. To keep herself from acting upon that wild impulse, she asked him how his uncle was doing. "I believe he expressed a desire to show Robbie to every servant on the place."

"True, but he stopped just short of taking the little boy down to be admired by the old fellow who tends the cows. In fact, Pimstock set a bevy of maids to cleaning the nursery, and when I saw Sir Allistair last, he was sitting beside Robbie's cot, watching the child sleep."

While Delia searched her mind for something else to ask, Mitchell began moving his fingertips up and down her arm—slowly, softly—sending shivers of delight all along her spine. *He must know he is doing that thing with his fingertips!*

When she stole a glace at his profile, and saw the corners of his lips twitch, as if he were trying to hide his amusement, all her doubts vanished. He knew exactly what he was doing! And unless she missed her guess, he knew exactly what it was doing to her!

He continued to look straight ahead, and while she stared at him, he licked his lips, puckered, and began to whistle a little Scottish tune she had known since she was a little girl. It was "Lassie, Will Ye Marry Me?"

"Mitchell! Do you know what you are whistling?"

He said not a word, and while she waited for his reply, her pride told her to get up and walk away. Fortunately, her heart told her to stay, for Mitchell turned and looked directly at her, his smile so warm it was like a physical touch, so warm she felt as if she might melt.

"Well, lassie? What say ye? Will ye marry me?"

Yes! Oh, yes! Delia wanted to say the words, but something stopped her. "Are you asking me because of what happened beneath the bridge? Out of some misguided sense of gratitude?"

He shook his head. "What I feel has nothing to do with gratitude."

"What is it, then? Surely you are not worried about having compromised me. I am no chit fresh from the schoolroom, and even if I were, I would still want no part of a forced—"

He silenced her in the time honored way, by covering her mouth with his own. "Foolish, foolish girl," he said, "I want to marry you because I love you with all my heart, and because I cannot imagine the rest of my life without you by my side."

"Truly?"

"Truly," he said. "Now, if I have answered all your questions, will you be so good as to answer mine?"

"Yes," she said. "I will marry you."

Happy to have her answer at last, he pulled her close against his chest. "I never dreamed I could love anyone as I love you," he whispered, "and I want you so badly I fear something calamitous may happen if I have to wait one more minute to taste your lips."

Delia felt certain they had endured enough misfortunes for one lifetime, and wanting no part of another one, she turned her face up to her beloved's and bid him taste to his heart's content.

About the Author

Martha Kirkland is a graduate of Georgia State University and a lifelong student of classical music. She shares a love of tennis with her husband and a love of the ocean with her two daughters. As a soldier in the war against illiteracy, she volunteers two afternoons a week as a tutor in a local middle school.

Martha loves to hear from her readers. Her e-mail address is talkirkland@mindspring.com.